S. ALICE CALLAHAN

WYNEMA
A Child of the Forest

"For right is right, since God is God,
And right the day must *win"*

Edited and Introduced by A. LaVonne Brown Ruoff

University of Nebraska Press, Lincoln and London

Publication of this volume was
assisted by The Virginia Faulkner
Fund, established in memory of
Virginia Faulkner, editor-in-chief of
the University of Nebraska Press.

Originally published in 1891 by H. J.
Smith and Company, Chicago.
New material © 1997 by the
University of Nebraska Press. All
rights reserved. Manufactured in the
United States of America. ⊚ The
paper in this book meets the
minimum requirements of American
National Standard for Information
Sciences – Permanence of Paper for
Printed Library Materials,
ANSI Z39. 48-1984. Library of
Congress Cataloging-in-Publication
Data. Callahan, S. Alice, b. 1868.
Wynema : a child of the forest /
by S. Alice Callahan.   p.   cm.
ISBN 0-8032-1460-X (cloth : alk.
paper). – ISBN 0-8032-6378-3
(pbk. : alk. paper) 1. Creek Indians –
Fiction. 2. Indian women – Fiction.
I. Title. PS1251.C36W96 1997
813'.4 – DC20 96-28385 CIP

S. Alice Callahan. Reprinted, by permission, from Carolyn Thomas Foreman, "S. Alice Callahan: Author of *Wynema, A Child of the Forest,*" *Chronicles of Oklahoma* 33, no.3 (autumn 1955), facing p.306. Copyright 1955 Oklahoma Historical Society, Oklahoma City.

TO THE INDIAN TRIBES OF NORTH AMERICA WHO HAVE FELT THE WRONGS AND OPPRESSION OF THEIR PALE-FACED BROTHERS, I LOVINGLY DEDICATE THIS WORK, PRAYING THAT IT MAY SERVE TO OPEN THE EYES AND HEART OF THE WORLD TO OUR AFFLICTIONS, AND THUS SPEEDILY ISSUE INTO EXISTENCE AN ERA OF GOOD FEELING AND JUST DEALING TOWARD US AND OUR MORE OPPRESSED BROTHERS.   *The Author*

CONTENTS

PUBLISHER'S PREFACE

In offering "Wynema" for your perusal, reader, the publishers have no apologies to offer for what literary critics may term the crudeness or the incompleteness of the work. The fact that an Indian, one of the oppressed, desires to plead her cause at a tribunal where judge and jury are chosen from among the oppressors is our warrant for publishing this little volume.

Honest opinions which come from careful thought and deep study are worthy of respectful consideration even though they be the opinions of an Indian, and whoever reads these pages will be convinced that this protest against the present Indian policy of our government is sincere, earnest, and timely.

The Red Men have not been without champions and defenders in the relentless war which the white man's greed has waged unceasingly against them since the landing of Columbus, yet never before, so far as we can learn, have our Red brothers had their story told by the pen of one of their own people. We shall claim then, for this little volume this: It is the Indians' side of the Indian question told by an Indian born and bred, and told none the less potently because the author has borrowed the garb of fiction to present the cause of truth. Her picture of the home-life of this simple people, of their customs and ceremonies, of their aspirations for higher life, of their inherent weaknesses, of their patient endurance of injustice, oppression and suffering, of their despair and hopelessness, of their last defiance of governmental authority, and of the magnificent results accomplished by those who have gone among them to teach and to preach is worthy of the reader's most careful attention.

CHICAGO, APRIL 1, 1891

ACKNOWLEDGMENTS

I am grateful to the staffs of the Oklahoma Historical Society, Oklahoma City, and the Newberry Library, Chicago, where research for this edition was done. Fellowships from the Institute for the Humanities, University of Illinois at Chicago, and the National Endowment for the Humanities greatly facilitated the preparation of this edition. A grant from the UIC Graduate College enabled me to purchase microfilms of Oklahoma Indian newspapers.

Daniel F. Littlefield Jr. generously sent a typescript of references to the Callahan family in Muskogee newspapers and quickly answered my many questions. Annette Van Dyke graciously provided a copy of the conclusion to *Wynema* missing from the Oklahoma Historical Society's copy. Alan Cook, historic preservation officer, Muscogee (Creek) Nation, provided invaluable comments on the manuscript. Michael Dorris kindly sent a copy of his "Modoc Sketches." For additional assistance, acknowledged in the notes, I am grateful to Frat E. Davis, Sulphur Springs, Texas; Susan M. Clark, Reference Department, Staunton Public Library, Virginia; Catharine Bushman, Staunton, Virginia; Beatrice Medicine; Harvey Markowitz, D'Arcy McNickle Center for the History of the American Indian, Newberry Library; Tim Thompson, language specialist, Muscogee (Creek) Nation; Annette B. Fromm, Creek Council House; Lauren Stuart Muller, doctoral student, University of California, Berkeley; and Alfred Epstein, librarian, Frances E. Willard Memorial Library, Evanston, Illinois.

EDITOR'S INTRODUCTION

Wynema (1891) by Sophia Alice Callahan (Muscogee [Creek], 1868–94) is probably the first novel written by a woman of American Indian descent.[1] The history of the Native American literature written in English begins in 1772 with the publication of Samson Occom's (Mohegan, 1723–92) *Sermon Preached at the Execution of Moses Paul, an Indian*. The first Native American woman to publish was Jane Johnston Schoolcraft (Ojibwe, 1800–41), whose poems, essays, and translations of Ojibwe legends appeared in *The Literary Voyager or Muzzenyegun,* a magazine her husband, Henry, produced with her assistance. Not until the late nineteenth and early twentieth centuries did other native women publish their work. Like their male counterparts, American Indian women authors such as Callahan, Sarah Winnemucca Hopkins (Paiute, c. 1844–91), Emily Pauline Johnson (Mohawk, 1861–1913), and Zitkala Ša (Gertrude Bonnin, Lakota Sioux, 1876–1938) described the impact of the dominant society on Indian life and culture. What distinguishes their work from that of native male writers is their added emphasis on the nature of women's roles.

Callahan was the daughter of Samuel Benton Callahan and Sarah Elizabeth Callahan. Samuel, one-eighth Muscogee, was very active in tribal affairs throughout his life. Born in 1833 in Alabama, Samuel was the son of Amanda Doyle (Muscogee) and James Oliver Callahan, an Irishman described variously as a well-known shipbuilder or architect from Pennsylvania. When Samuel was three, his family migrated from Eufaula, Alabama, to Indian Territory. His father died of privation and exposure during the journey. Subsequently the family settled in

This edition is for Joy Harjo and all the other Muscogee writers.

Sulphur Springs, Texas, near Dallas, where Samuel completed his public education. In 1856, he left McKenzie College in Clarksville, Texas, to edit the *Sulphur Springs Gazette*. He and Sarah Elizabeth McAllester were married in 1858. The next year he established the headquarters of his cattle ranch near Okmulgee, Indian Territory, but his operations ranged over a considerable area.[2]

Although he owned many slaves before the Civil War, Samuel opposed slavery. An ardent believer in states' rights, he enlisted in 1861 in the First Creek Mounted Volunteers of the Confederate Army. In the spring, shortly after Samuel left, a band of marauders pillaged and burned his trading post and stripped his house. Carrying a bag of gold and accompanied by two Callahan children and a slave nurse, Sarah fled to Sulphur Springs. It was twenty years before Sarah could be persuaded to return to Indian Territory.

In 1862, Samuel was elected as a member of the Confederate Congress at Richmond and, in 1863, became captain of Company K of the First Creek Confederate Regiment. The next year he was again a delegate to the Confederate Congress. After his return to Sulphur Springs in 1865, Samuel became a merchant. Within a year, he moved to Indian Territory to become a farmer and stock raiser near Muskogee. He amassed a second fortune, only to see it swept away when the "blackleg" disease killed three thousand of his cattle in a single season. His family apparently remained in Sulphur Springs. From 1868 to 1872, Samuel served as a clerk in the Muscogee House of Kings, their equivalent of the United States Senate. During this period, Samuel lived in Okmulgee, the tribal capital. Not until 1885 did he move his family permanently to Indian Territory. Samuel purchased a hotel in Okmulgee, which the *Indian Journal* (Eufaula, Creek Nation) reported on 5 November 1885 was crowded with guests during the Council session (4.3). After

Samuel became editor of the *Indian Journal* in Muskogee, the family moved there in 1886 or in 1887.

Later Samuel became clerk of the Muscogee Nation's supreme court and, in 1901, a justice of this court. He served as executive secretary to three principal chiefs of the Muscogee Nation: Samuel Checote, Roly McIntosh (acting chief), and Isparhecher. On many occasions he was a tribal delegate to negotiations in Washington DC. Deeply interested in Indian education, Samuel served as superintendent of the Wealaka Boarding School from 1892 to 1894. This Methodist mission school was located on the Arkansas River in the Coweta District of the Muscogee Nation and southeast of present-day Tulsa. Before he died in 1911, Samuel was the last living member of the Confederate States Congress at Richmond. He was buried in his Confederate uniform.

The Callahans were members of the Muscogee aristocracy, described by the *Muskogkee Times Democrat* ("Capt. Callahan Dies Here Today" 17 February 1911) as rich in gold or stock and in control of Muscogee politics. Black slaves tilled their land and herded their cattle while they rode in carriages. To adorn their homes, they shipped pianos and mahogany furniture up the Mississippi and Arkansas Rivers. "When their women bought a new dress the whole bolt of cloth was taken to make sure that no other woman secured a similar pattern." This wealth made their ranches and plantations "magnificent plunder" for the marauders who, during the Civil War, drove off the women and killed the old men that the fighting men left behind (3.1–2). In *The Road to Disappearance*, Angie Debo paints a similar picture of mixed-blood life. Most lived in the eastern portion of the Muscogee Nation, residing in great ranch houses or comfortable town residences built in Eufaula and later to an increasing extent in Tulsa and Muskogee. "They were proud of their Indian blood and sympathetic toward the real Indians, and they formed a closely-knit but kindly aristocracy" (285). They owned trading houses in the towns, operated great farms, and, most of all, joined in the recent development of the ranching industry.

Little is known about the life of Alice, born in 1868 in Sulphur Springs, where she spent the first seventeen years of her life.[3] By 1886 she apparently was teaching in Okmulgee, Indian Territory; the *Indian Journal* reported on 20 May that the school there was in "a flourishing condition" under her management (4.2). She attended the Wesleyan Female Institute in Staunton, Virginia, for ten months, returning on 14 June 1888. This gracious institute, undoubtedly the model for Keithly College in *Wynema*, specialized in a liberal arts education. The four basic departments of education were physical, intellectual, social, and religious. A business school was added in 1881.[4] Announcing the return of Alice and Lotti Edwards, the *Indian Journal* enthused on 21 June 1888 that "these young ladies won honors of rare merit in that institute as a reward of persevering effort and close application, for which they deserved the congratulations of parents and friends" (5.1).

In February 1891, Callahan became a teacher at Muskogee's Harrell International Institute, a private Methodist high school established in 1882 by authority of the Muscogee Council.[5] Its goal was to teach Indian and white children "elements of sciences and agriculture and mechanical arts" (Foreman, *Muscogee* 52–54). In 1891, Callahan became an editor of *Our Brother in Red*, a Methodist journal associated with Harrell. By that time, the journal's regular "Temperance" column, begun in 1888, was dominated by news of the activities of the Women's Christian Temperance Union (Littlefield and Parins 291). In spring 1891, Callahan completed *Wynema*. On 6 June, *Our Brother in Red* announced the publication of the novel: "[Callahan] is an intelligent christian lady and we look forward with pleasure to a time when our other duties will permit us to read the book. It is certainly cheap at 25 cents per copy" (4.1). Unfortunately, this left-handed compliment was one of the only notices the book received. Newspapers in Oklahoma and Chicago, where *Wynema* was published, ignored the book. Its publication was one of the few bright spots in a difficult year. Callahan's fifty-two-year-old mother, an invalid for many months, died in October.[6] In 1892, during a revival of religion in the Muskogee Methodist church, Callahan evidently "gave her self more fully to God."[7]

In 1892 and 1893, she taught at Wealaka School. This large, three-story building, planned for one hundred pupils, opened in 1882 to replace the burned Tullahassee Mission. Her own letters and those written by her friends offer glimpses of her life and interests during this period. On 4 September 1892, she wrote a friend from Muskogee that the staff had been very busy at the school, cleaning house and drying fruit. When a wagonload of people arrived, she had to cook and serve supper for seventeen people, besides the family. In this letter she also discussed her literary tastes. Callahan was reading *Vanity Fair,* which amused and entertained her more than anything she had read, though she had been more interested in Lytton and Dickens. Her reaction to some of Thackeray's comments reflects her feminism expressed in *Wynema.*

It is so satirical and treats the world so much as a fair in which the words, actions and feelings of the dramatis personae are exhibited without excuse or comment. In fact it is just such a book as I would expect from the pen of Thackeray. I don't like a great many things he says such as "it's only women who get together and hiss and shriek and cackle," or "the best of women are hypocrits—A good house wife is of necessity a humbug. (qtd. in Foreman, "S. Alice Callahan" 312)

Both Samuel and Callahan wanted her to complete her education. In February 1893, she wrote that her father was anxious for her to return to Staunton the next year to finish her schooling:

I think it best to go there [Wesleyan Female Institute] to finish as I have begun there. I am studying on my French & Mathematics, preparing if I go back I shall study nothing but languages & literature & Mathematics. I finished Latin but I shall study it again. . . . When I finish I am going to build up a school of my own. We have an excellent French teacher at Staunton, and have also a French table where nothing but French is allowed to be spoken. (qtd. in a letter from Lulu Todd to Ruby Fears, 7 January 1894, in Foreman, "S. Alice Callahan" 312; see also Foreman, "S. Alice Callahan" 313 n.13)

In a letter dated 10 April 1893, Callahan wrote that she was very busy teaching children marches and songs in addition to choruses and instrumental music. She was also training girls for their recitations in competition for a prize. Callahan took on additional duties when she was elected correspondence secretary of the Conference Officers of Parsonages and Home Mission Society at the forty-eighth session of the Indian Mission Conference, Methodist Episcopal Church, South, which convened in Vinita, Cherokee Nation, on 1 November.[8]

Despite her desire to complete her schooling, Callahan was back at Harrell by December to complete the term of a sick teacher. In a letter dated 7 December the author described how happy she was with her teaching and her colleagues:

I am right well pleased too. My classes are much more interesting & pleasanter than they were before. I have four I like real well: I e, Mental philosophy, Mythology, Physics, Geography and Algebra. . . . We have a much nicer set of girls than we have ever had before and I think we have more pretty girls than I ever remember before. And the teachers! Oh that's just the best of all! They are so nice. (qtd. in Foreman, "S. Alice Callahan" 313)

While traveling to Muskogee from Wealaka, Callahan told her father that she felt as if she was going to die. An acute attack of pleurisy on 26 December 1893 cut short her teaching career and her plans to finish her education. After considerable suffering, she died on 7 January 1894, at the age of twenty-six. In a loving tribute published on 11 January, *Our Brother in Red* praised her "literary turn of mind" and her abilities as a teacher, which had never been "excelled in this territory."[9]

THE NOVEL

An acculturated, well-read, and independent daughter of a father actively involved in tribal affairs, Callahan was well aware of the injustices endured by both Indians and women. Because of her mixed-blood heritage and education, she was both part of and separate from the Muscogee people, culture, and issues she examines. In *Wynema*, Callahan uses a double-voiced discourse, which simultaneously expresses the direct intention of the character speaking and the refracted intention of the author.[10] The speeches of Callahan's characters represent not only the intention of character and author but also two cultures, Indian and non-Indian, and two genders, male and female. *Wynema* demonstrates how Indian women authors used and departed from literary trends present in nineteenth-century women's literature.

That the author's purpose in writing *Wynema* is to arouse her readers' anger about the outrages perpetrated against Indians is clear from her dedication of the book "to the Indian tribes of North America, who have felt the wrongs and oppression of their pale-faced brothers." The plot focuses on the acculturation and romances of two heroines, Genevieve Weir, a non-Indian Methodist teacher from a genteel Southern family, and Wynema Harjo, a full-blood Muscogee child who becomes her best student and dear friend.[11]

The first section of the novel chronicles Genevieve's adjustments to life as a Methodist teacher in the Muscogee Nation. Wynema and Gerald Keithly, a Methodist missionary, help her to understand Muscogee culture. The first section also describes the "civilizing" of Wynema. A reverse acculturation theme is introduced in chapter 11, when Genevieve takes Wynema on a visit to the Weirs' home, where the heroines must adjust or readjust to Southern lifestyles. Genevieve, who has turned down Gerald's proposal because she has an "understanding" with Maurice Mauran, a childhood friend, breaks off the relationship when she realizes how prejudiced this Southern gentleman is against Indians and women. She then accepts Gerald's proposal. In the meantime, Wynema and Robin Weir, Genevieve's sensitive and enlightened brother, fall in love. Both women return to the Muscogee Nation, where they subsequently marry their beloveds. Two other romances, involving Genevieve's younger sisters, are briefly introduced but not developed: between Bessie Weir and Carl Peterson, a missionary to the Muscogees who formerly served the Lakota Sioux, and between Winnie Weir and a Dr. Bradford. The last section tests our "willing suspension of disbelief" as Carl and Robin rush off to the Sioux Nation during the hostilities of late 1890 that led to the massacre at Wounded Knee on 29 December.

Callahan's own bicultural background, years in Staunton, experiences as a teacher at Methodist mission school for Muscogees, and staunch support for women's rights and suffrage inform the novel. She uses a plot formula that Nina Baym, in *Women's Fiction,* indicates was common in America from 1820 to 1870: women fiction writers chronicled the "trials and triumph" of a "heroine, who, beset with hardships, finds within herself the qualities of intelligence, will, resourcefulness, and courage sufficient to overcome them" (17).[12] That Callahan was influenced by this formula is clear from her description of Genevieve as "physically unfit to bear the hardships of life among the Indians" but nevertheless endowed by God with "great moral courage and endurance." Both intelligent and pretty, Genevieve possesses "the graces of heart and head" and has been "surrounded by the luxuries of a Southern home." Unpersuaded by her mother's tearful pleas that she stay home, Genevieve leaves her family to become a teacher to the Muscogees. At a time when few women, especially Southern women, left home on their own before marriage, Genevieve's decision reveals considerable independence.[13] However, by providing Genevieve with a husband who more than equals her in kindness and dedication, Callahan keeps her heroine within the boundaries that Larzer Ziff points out were characteristic of that decade. Many a determined daughter in this period sought economic independence "not just to show that she could compete equally with men, but to protect the sanctity of her inner nature. Her dream was to enter into marriage or other relations with men as an equal party whose demands were to be respected every bit as much as the demands the male's nature made upon him" (278).

Callahan's blending of domestic romance with discussions of women's and Indians' rights is consistent with the traditions of sentimental fiction, which Jane Tompkins describes as a move toward a greater scope and democratization that is profoundly a "political enterprise, halfway between sermon and social theory, that both codifies and attempts to mold the values of its time" (123, 126; cf. Douglas). Lauren Berlent suggests that nineteenth-century sentimental activists charged themselves "and their sister women with the dual aim of social amelioration and change" (269). A growing body of evidence suggests, according to Peggy Pasco, that Victorian female reformers fought against male privilege even as they defended the Christian home. Especially relevant to the plot of *Wynema* is the concept of this home advocated by women in the home mission movement, who envisioned a Christian home "centered around the moral authority of the wife rather than the patriarchal control of the husband." For home mission women in the late nineteenth century, "female 'submission' was no longer a mark of true womanhood." Implicit in their concept of the Christian home was a deep concern for improving the status of women. Home mission women developed among themselves a version of history in which female emancipation was the logical outcome of Christianization (36, 40, 44).

Although Callahan's heroines and heroes possess the characteristics traditional to domestic romance, they are also strong-hearted women of ideas and gentle men sensitive to Indians' and women's issues. Genevieve's nurturing, maternal side is revealed in her relationship with Wynema. However, she is also a complex domestic heroine—at once a shy romantic longing for love and a strong-minded, independent woman wary of marriage. To portray what Callahan obviously feels is the ideal love—one that grows out of mutual respect between intelligent men and women—she provides Genevieve with two lovers who behave very differently toward women. Gerald Keithly, a Methodist missionary, is a gentle, quiet, sympathetic man while Maurice Mauran is a bullying bigot equally prejudiced against Indians and self-sufficient women. Genevieve is shocked by his "old-fogy" opinions that women should not have any ideas "except about housekeeping, fancy-work, dress and society, until after they are married, when they only echo the opinions of their husbands." He regards women's rights as "immodest and unwomanly." An angry Genevieve retorts that "the idea of a woman being unwomanly and immodest because she happens to be thoughtful and to have 'two ideas above an oyster,' to know a little beyond and above house and dress is perfectly absurd and untrue." She interrupts his later tirade against Indians with a fiery speech: "I asked you for an opinion; you have given me vituperation; and not being content with slandering the poor, ignorant, defenseless Indians, you begin on me." After attacking him for his inability to "understand the first principles of logic," Genevieve breaks their engagement.

Another domestic romance between a woman of ideas and a sensitive man is that between Wynema and Robin Weir, Genevieve's younger brother. An exceptionally bright and determined child, Wynema exemplifies the possibilities of acculturating Indians through education. Unlike the other full-blood children, who had to be enticed into learning, Wynema is a quick student who "learns faster and retains more of what she learns, than any child of whatever hue" Genevieve has ever known. By the time she visits Genevieve's home in the South, Wynema has become a cultured, refined young lady who speaks fluent English and whose personal qualities endear her to the Weir family. The relationship between Wynema and Robin exemplifies the true, respectful love that can be achieved both between educated and right-thinking adults and between an Indian woman and a white man. Like her role model, Genevieve, Wynema is an informed woman of ideas who argues her positions in spirited debate. Both women are staunch supporters of equal rights for women, reflecting Callahan's strong support of this movement, which gained strength in the 1890s.[14] With clear irony, Wynema states her firm belief that one day " 'the inferior of man,' the 'weaker vessel' shall stand grandly by the side of that 'noble lord of creation,' his equal in *every* respect." She emphasizes that the idea of freedom and liberty was born in her, not something she learned from Genevieve. Although she confesses that Muscogee women have no voice in the councils and do not speak in any public gathering or in churches, Wynema proclaims that "we are waiting for our more civilized white sisters to gain their liberty, and thus set us an example which we shall not be slow to follow." With the political correctness essential for Wynema's future husband, Robin expresses his wholehearted support: "There is no man who is enterprising and keeps well up with the times but confesses that the women of to-day are in every respect, except political liberty, equal to the men."

Callahan emphasizes her heroines' intelligence by having them carry on conversations about such important political issues as the allotment of Muscogee land in severalty under the 1887 Dawes Act or Muscogee political corruption, demonstrating that female conversation was not limited to concerns of the home or gossip. That these proud, articulate women have chosen their husbands wisely is demonstrated by the scenes of domestic bliss at the Keithly home. Genevieve and Gerald, though parents, are "happy lovers still," while Wynema is beautified by time.

The final section of the novel, devoted to hostilities in the Sioux nation, provides Callahan with an opportunity to create an idealized portrait of traditional Indian marriage. The defiant, proud warrior Wildfire vainly tries to persuade his wife, Miscona, and other warriors' wives to return to the reservation. Instead, the forty loyal women choose to accompany their men into battle and die with them if necessary. Wildfire and Miscona die in battle, locked in each others' arms. Callahan undoubtedly creates this portrait of a loving Indian marriage to humanize the impact of the conflict on the Sioux.

Callahan undercuts the stereotypical plot of the plucky white heroine who risks life and limb to bring education and religion to "savage heathens" by beginning the novel with a description of the Muscogees' Edenic life in a virgin landscape and by her characterization of the warm family relationship between Wynema and her doting father, Choe Harjo. Although the traditional Muscogees in the novel do engage in "barbaric" practices that offend Genevieve's sensibilities, these friendly "savages" are far too noble for the reader to fear that they would harm a hair on Genevieve's pious head. Most of the first section introduces Genevieve and the reader to Muscogee customs and beliefs. Callahan's vivid descriptions of Genevieve's negative reactions to some aspects of Muscogee life reveal some of the author's own ambivalence as an acculturated Muscogee. Although Callahan is careful to defend the tribe's tastes and customs, sometimes her depictions of Genevieve's repulsion are more convincing than her justifications. One of the more obvious examples is Genevieve's reaction to "sofky," a favorite Muscogee dish made from dried hominy, which Callahan describes as palatable when fresh but preferred by Indians "after it has soured and smells more like a swill-barrel than anything else."

Callahan uses multiple voices and perspectives, Indian and non-Indian, female and male, to educate her readers. Gerald Keithly is the author's major spokesperson to explain the significance of Muscogee customs. Presumably, Callahan uses him because Wynema is too young and unskilled in English in the first section of the novel to engage in extended discourse with her teacher and because Gerald, as an educated and sympathetic white man, might be more convincing than a Muscogee to white audiences. One such discourse occurs when Genevieve, amazed by the Muscogee "busk" or Green Corn Dance, vehemently says that Indians should quit these "barbaric customs," to which they cling "no matter how much they associate with whites." Gerald explains, with ironic humor, that the "busk" is more civilized than the galas held by whites because Indians choose more sensible places for their dances than do whites, their "squaws" dress more modestly, and they dance only a few times a year, unlike whites who dance every night during "the season." After observing a Muscogee ritual, Genevieve asks whether Gerald only encourages the Indians to keep up their "barbaric customs" when he participates in their "strange ceremonies." Clearly expressing Callahan's point of view, Gerald firmly replies that the Muscogees should be allowed to keep the ceremonies that do no harm: "These Indians have long ago laid aside their savage, cruel customs and have no more desire to practice them than we have to see them do so."

The third section, on Sioux hostilities, the murder of Sitting Bull, and the massacre at Wounded Knee, is such an abrupt departure from the earlier romance plot that it was probably added to an almost completed novel. The picture of domestic bliss, in which the married Wynema and Genevieve are surrounded by their loved ones and live in harmony with the Muscogees, is interrupted when Carl announces he must rejoin his Sioux friends, who are about to go to war. Accompanied by Robin, Carl acts as an intermediary between Sioux chiefs and the army. In the final chapter, Callahan combines the themes of domestic romance and protest novel: Carl and Robin have returned from the Sioux hostilities accompanied by an old Sioux woman and three orphaned infants, one of whom Carl plans to raise. Gerald Keithly and Wynema want the other two. Here Callahan contrasts the love and security of Genevieve's and Wynema's family circles with the cruelty of the massacre at Wounded Knee and a strong statement about the government's unjust treatment of Indians.

Like the romance authors of the age, Callahan often creates sentimental scenes and uses stilted language. Her introductory chapter, which presents the idyllic life of the Muscogees in Indian Territory before white encroachment, exemplifies her sometimes melodramatic style: "Ah, happy, peaceable Indians! Here you may dream of the happy hunting-grounds beyond, little thinking of the rough, white hand that will soon shatter your dream and scatter the dreams." In scenes between Robin Weir and Wynema and between Genevieve and Gerald Keithly, Callahan creates enough male passion and female repressed sexuality to titillate but not shock her readers. Both women subordinate their emotions to propriety. After he proposes, Robin tries to kiss Wynema, who turns away, admonishing him; " 'When we are married,' flushing at the word, 'will be soon enough.' " She flees after he embraces and kisses her repeatedly. Later reading his letter of apology while alone in her room, Wynema kisses it before putting it away. Scenes between Genevieve and Gerald, following the women's return to Muscogee territory, reveal a similar pattern. When Genevieve tries to stop him from once more declaring his love, Gerald pleads; "Now let me free the love that has been barred up so long. Oh, my darling, I hope you may never know what heart-hunger is!" Gerald extracts from Genevieve her promise to let him know if she changes her mind about marrying him. However, Callahan does not dwell on such scenes. Immediately after this conversation, the not-quite lovers join others to discuss allotment. In the scene in which Genevieve finally admits her love for Gerald, Callahan depicts her as both a shy, traditional romantic heroine and a tease. When Gerald asks if she has anything to say now, she reminds him about Maurice Mauran. The love-struck missionary then asks if she can not "love me the least bit in the world." Genevieve first whispers "No" to the disappointed Gerald before she finally surrenders: " 'Don't you know? Because I love you *more* than *that*,' and she gave him one sweet look out of her soft, love-bedewed eyes."

Callahan's style is also full of literary and Biblical allusions. Among the authors and hymn writers whom she refers to or quotes are Cicero, Shakespeare, Milton, Gray, Pope, Scott, Byron, Tennyson, Dickens, Friedrich Halm as translated by Maria Lovell, Frederick William Faber, and Whittier. Her allusions reveal her preference for nineteenth-century British writers. Like many religious writers of the period, she embeds numerous Biblical quotations, which emphasize the piety of her characters.

The most interesting dimension of the novel's style is Callahan's use of Muscogee dialect, primarily in young Wynema's dialogue. Humorists as far back as the 1830s used dialect, as Daniel F. Littlefield Jr. notes in his fine introduction to Alexander Posey's *Fus Fixico Letters*. Territorial newspapers published works by well-known dialect humorists and many Indian Territory writers imitated these earlier forms and styles. During the 1880s, "territorial writers established a tradition of dialect humor that grew in popularity within the next twenty years" (Littlefield 23). Muscogee writers such as Posey and

Charles Gibson skillfully used Muscogee dialect in their satire. Gibson called this "este charte" or "red man" English. Both Posey and Gibson condemned bad imitations of Muscogee dialect. Littlefield emphasizes that Posey's "este charte" dialect, unlike that of imitators, uses the verb *to be* to determine tense, nominative personal pronouns as reflexives or possessives, and the expression *maybe so* to indicate conditional action or possibility (18).

Callahan uses varied language and dialect to depict full-blood Muscogees in the novel. She first introduces Wynema and her father, Choe Harjo, in a scene in which they undoubtedly converse in Muscogee. To demonstrate their fluency and literacy in that language, Callahan renders this dialogue in fairly formal, grammatical English. She primarily reserves dialect for young Wynema's conversations with Gerald and Genevieve. Gerald always speaks English to Wynema because she is young and "can readily acquire a new language." The little girl's attempts to converse in English are exemplified by her comment on why blue dumplings are so dark: "It is the burn shells; we burn it an' put in the meal an' it makes it blue. Goot! eat some, Mihia. It is so goot." Another example is the child's statement to Genevieve that everyone is going to the busk: "We go busk 'night. Eferypoty, no school, you go—nopoty stay with you—all go busk." That Wynema's mother speaks a more heavily inflected English is clear from her reaction to hearing that Genevieve is sick: " 'Seek?' questioned the mother. 'What eat?' " Callahan uses Wynema's dialect to indicate both her limited knowledge of English as a child and her youth. The girl's Muscogee-style English disappears forever on the page where she and Genevieve discuss her proposed trip to the teacher's Southern home. Although Wynema is now mature and educated enough to become Genevieve's friend rather than her pupil, the young Muscogee woman continues to call her friend "Mihia" (teacher) until she marries Robin.

Callahan does not follow some of the language patterns that Posey used. To reproduce "este charte" dialect, Callahan relies mainly on imitations of Muscogee pronunciation of English and sentence structure. She omits articles, the word *to* as a preposition or part of an infinitive, verb endings that indicate number and tense, and parts of words and sentences. Though we do not know whether or to what extent Callahan knew the Muscogee language, she was familiar with the "este charte" English used by her students at Wealaka Mission School. Her reports for the third and fourth quarters of 1893 indicate that approximately two-thirds of her students understood and spoke English. She describes in chapter 2, "The School," Genevieve's problems with communicating to her students and their parents. The heroine's vow to teach the children ancient and modern languages and higher mathematics is not as idealistic as it may appear. Callahan herself taught Latin, algebra, and natural philosophy, among other subjects, to her Wealaka pupils in 1893.[15]

In the sections on the Sioux hostilities, Callahan uses fluent, forceful language rather than dialect in the dialogues between Carl Peterson, Wildfire, and Great Eye and between Wildfire and Miscona. The eloquent, grammatical speeches of the Sioux suggest the power of the Lakota language. Old Chikena uses the same type of language to describe the massacre of her people to the ever-precocious Wynema, who learned Lakota as a child, from an old Sioux woman living with the Harjos. The Sioux characters' use of *pale-face* indicates differences between Indians and non-Indians more than differences in dialect because Callahan herself uses the term in her descriptions and in some of the dialogue by characters such as Gerald Keithly.

The Muscogee or Creek Nation, now situated in southeastern Oklahoma, was formerly located in present-day Alabama and Georgia. The Muscogees called their nation Is-te-cm-us-suk-c-kee or "people of the Holly Leaf Confederacy," from the Gulf holly used in their ceremonials. They were divided into many matrilineal clans. According to their oral history, the Muscogees came from the west and migrated toward the sunrise, crossing a great and muddy river, before settling in their eastern home. After contact, the Muscogee alliance increased its power and doubled its population by incorporating defeated tribes (Debo 3. See also Champagne; Green; Martin).

Muscogees recognized peace and war as separate governmental functions, classifying towns as White or Peace towns and Red or War towns. Generally located on a river or creek, these towns were often surrounded by smaller villages. The leading men of the town assembled every day in council at the square. The head of the government was the *micco* or "town chief." Private dwellings of each town were grouped around a public place, consisting of the *chunkey* yard, a sunken rectangle with banks for spectators; the *chokofa*, used for councils and meetings held in bad weather; and the square, the political and ceremonial meeting place during the summer.

White settlers first established plantations in Muscogee territory in 1733. Fifty years later, what became a long history of large cessions of Muscogee land began when the royal governor of Georgia demanded that the nation cede two million acres on the upper Savannah River as payment for trade debts. A crucial turning point in the Muscogee's efforts to hold on to their decreasing land base was the Red Stick War of 1813–14, when a small group of Muscogees took up Tecumseh's vision of uniting Indians to drive out the settlers.[16] In response to rebel attacks, the Muscogee Council ordered the execution of the offenders, and forces of outraged settlers invaded Muscogee territory.Though the rebels retreated to Seminole territory in Florida, the war broke the spirit of the Muscogees.

The Muscogees felt strongly about retaining their land, as Callahan makes clear in her description of how a Muscogee leader was killed for selling land without council approval. In 1811, on the advice of William McIntosh, a mixed blood, the Council imposed the death penalty for any chief authorizing unapproved land sales. Muscogees continued to cede land until, in 1824, the Council declared it would sell no more. Nevertheless, McIntosh, Etommee Tustennuggee, thirteen lesser chiefs, and about fifty other men signed the Treaty of Indian Springs, selling all Muscogee land in Georgia and the northern two-thirds of Alabama in exchange for a wild western tract. McIntosh later signed a supplementary treaty assuring him twenty-five thousand dollars for his residence and 1,640 acres of improved land in a ceded tract. The Council pronounced a death sentence on McIntosh and his collaborators. Avengers set fire to McIntosh's house and then shot him and Etommee Tustennuggee as they attempted to escape. Others associated with McIntosh were shot or hanged. The Muscogee Council issued a formal statement declaring that it only enforced its own laws. Resolved to refuse all payments under the illegal treaty, the Council vowed to refrain from war against "those who should be sent to take their land from them" and to "die at the corners of their fences, . . . rather than . . . abandon the land of their forefathers" (qtd. in Debo 90).

By 1827, the Muscogees agreed to cede the rest of their land in Georgia and, in 1832, surrendered all of their land in Alabama. Between 1834 and 1836, 2,495 Muscogees were forcibly removed to Indian Territory, where, after much suffering, they gradually established communities. Their peaceful life was interrupted in 1861, when the Grand Council of United Nations of Indian Territory signed a treaty with the Confederate government, giving free passage to Confederate troops and authority to call on member nations for troops to repel Union forces. Muscogees loyal to the Union declared the treaty illegal and the office of chief vacant. Some raided the farms and establishments of the Callahans and other Confederate sympathizers. Like other tribes that supported the Confederate cause, the Muscogees lost additional land under the 1866 Treaty of Cession and Indemnity.

The two Muscogee factions agreed in 1867 to live as one nation, with a principal chief. They later wrote a constitution and code of laws and created a Council consisting of a House of Kings and a House of Warriors. After Removal, each town had retained its chief and other officers, chosen according to its custom from clan membership. Some towns elected their chiefs to the House of Kings. Members of this body, if they were not chiefs, often assumed responsibility for matters pertaining to the central government. Although Muscogee settlements laid out ceremonial grounds according to their own convenience, after the constitution was adopted, the Council decided what constituted a town. Civil conflict broke out in 1879 when a disaffected group supported a rival government. Anger over administration of justice, especially strong in the full-blood settlements in the hills west of Okmulgee, erupted into the Green Peach War, so named after soldiers helped themselves to the fruit of the orchards in an African American settlement. By the middle of August 1881, the insurrection was broken. Callahan does not allude to the factionalism that divided Muscogees during and after the Civil War or to this rebellion.

Although Callahan provides no dates in her novel, the correlation between Wynema's probable age and events in the Muscogee Nation suggest that *Wynema* is set in the period from the mid or late 1870s through 1890, when homesteaders increasingly moved onto Muscogee land. The action of the novel moves from what Callahan describes as the happy, peaceful time when full bloods dwelt in a village of tents far from the nearest trading point through the bustling period when tents have been replaced by "neat residences," a church has been built, and the village has grown to the point of wanting to have a name and a post office. Callahan's depiction of the Muscogees as dwelling in tepees when the action of the novel begins is a romantic evocation of Plains Indian dwellings rather than an accurate description of dwellings built by tribal members after Removal. By the 1880s Muscogees commonly inhabited cabins and mixed bloods often lived in larger residences. More accurate is her description of the replacement of the log-cabin school by a large frame building "constructed from the most approved modern plan and furnished with every convenience"; attendance has increased so much that Wynema is hired as a second teacher. This growth reflects the changes in Muscogee territory during the 1880s, and the changes in the school recall the building of Wealaka in 1882. To accommodate demands that more Indian land be opened to settlement, in 1885 Congress authorized the purchase of more land from Muscogees and Seminoles and of the Outlet, adjacent to the Cherokee Nation in northeastern Indian Territory, from the Cherokees. By this date, Muscogee land was occupied by cattlemen, who divided and built on the range as if they owned it.

Opposed to this sale, councils of the Five Civilized Tribes and neighboring tribes tried to draw up a constitution for an Indian confederation. They also opposed the passage of the Dawes Act of 1887, which allotted Indian land in severalty. In 1893, leaders of the Five Civilized Tribes refused to meet with the Dawes Commission to discuss allotment. The Muscogee Council in 1894 declined the propositions of this commission.

Consequently Congress delegated to the Dawes Commission authority to prepare rolls unilaterally and proceed with allotment. Although in 1897 the Choctaws and Chickasaws signed an agreement providing for allotment of their land to tribal citizens, the Muscogees, Seminoles, and Cherokees continued negotiations and delayed signing an agreement. Consequently, Congress passed the Curtis Act in 1898, requiring citizens of abolished Indian nations to submit to allotment. Under this act, Muscogee townsites were sold and their financial administration and their schools were placed under the control of the secretary of the interior. Their tribal affairs were liquidated by the Dawes Commission, partly under these provisions and partly under special agreements subsequently made with the Muscogee Nation.

Tribal resistance to forced allotment was led by Chitto Harjo (Crazy Snake), a full blood, and his followers, whom non-Indians called "Snakes." Harjo reestablished traditional tribal government, insisted that Muscogee treaties with the United States had granted lands to the Muscogee Nation in perpetuity, and affirmed the Muscogee Nation's right to self-government, regardless of congressional legislation. Finally, anti-allotment forces realized that resistance was futile. The Muscogees signed their allotment agreement in 1901. The Seminoles signed their allotment agreement in 1898 and the Cherokees, in 1902 (Gibson 502–4, Debo 372–73).[17]

In chapter 13, "Shall We Allot?," Callahan summarizes arguments for and against allotment expressed in Muscogee newspapers. Wynema staunchly advocates the allotment of Muscogee territory, to give Indians a pride in their own land that will encourage them to become farmers rather than continue living as hunters and fishers. Nevertheless, she finally acknowledges the validity of Genevieve's argument that allotment will be "the ruin of the poor, ignorant savage." Genevieve also warns that the Muscogees should never consent until their "weaker brothers are willing and able" because they will lose their lands and homes. A writer named "Wing" expressed similar sentiments in the 14 November 1889 issue of the *Indian Journal*. Emphasizing that most of the good land is occupied by whites, he calls allotment "ruinous to the last degree to the Indian." He concludes that "the Indian is not ready for this radical change, and we can not see any promise of his being so ready for many generations yet to come" (4.4, 8.1). As acculturated Muscogees, both Callahan and Wing argue against allotment because they feel traditional Muscogees lack what the dominant society defines as "education" and the experience necessary to fight off non-Indians' attempts to take Muscogee land by legal and illegal means. They imply that allotment can only be successful when Muscogees abandon their tribal culture and traditional way of life.

What Callahan and Wing ignore in their protective or "progressive" approach is that the strength of the Muscogee Nation had always come from its traditional social, religious, and cultural institutions. Throughout the Muscogees' history, these institutions functioned effectively, and they remained strong among the traditionals during the allotment period. The U.S. government's allotment of tribal lands in severalty and abolition of tribal governments were severe blows to the traditional social structure of the Muscogees and other Indian nations. Genevieve's and Wing's predictions about the impact of allotment on Native Americans proved all too true. Wilcomb E. Washburn estimates that by 1934 Native Americans had lost over 60 percent of the land they owned in 1887 (242–43).

New railroads and highways brought increasing numbers of traders and settlers into Muscogee territory. With the railroads and traders came the problem of controlling the liquor traffic. Despite enacting a "prohibition law" in 1882, Muscogees received scant support from the federal government or the courts during the 1890s in their efforts to control the sale of alcohol by traders in railroad towns. Callahan, a member of the Women's Christian Temperance Union in Muskogee, describes the disastrous effects of the liquor trade in Indian Territory. She correctly notes it was against federal law to bring alcohol onto Indian land. Under the 1802 Indian Trade and Intercourse Act, section 21, the president was authorized to take whatever steps deemed necessary "to prevent or restrain the vending or distribution of spirituous liquors among all or any of the said Indian tribes" (qtd. in Tyler, 41–42). Organized crime also increased in the Muscogee Nation during this period.

The Muscogees were also coping with misuse of tribal funds. Callahan describes in chapter 8, "What Became of It," the controversy of 1889 over disbursal of per capita funds. The controversey stemmed from the Muscogees' discovery in 1878 that they had unwittingly ceded an additional 151,870.48 acres of the western half of their land than was required under the terms of the 1866 Treaty of Cession and Indemnity. The Muscogees sought payment from the U.S. government for the additional acres, but because the land was to be set aside for use by other Indians and freed slaves, the Muscogees sold it for thirty cents an acre. In 1884, Congress appropriated $45,561.14 to pay for the land at this rate. The next year the Muscogees also received $41,004.90 as interest accrued during the period they had been deprived of their income from the sale of the land. Muscogee delegates Pleasant Porter, David M. Hodge, and Isparhecher made an unauthorized contract with Samuel J. Crawford of Kansas, who earlier had represented them in the matter of excess acreage, to negotiate an absolute cession to the United States. In March, Congress passed a law authorizing the purchase.

Because the land was to be opened to white settlement rather than reserved for Indians and freed slaves, the Muscogees negotiated in fall 1888 to increase the purchase price to $1.25 per acre. In January 1889, Congress signed and the Muscogee Council ratified this agreement. The tribe received an additional $2,280,857 for this land, $2 million of which was to be retained by the U.S. government to draw interest. Only $280,857 was to be turned over to the Muscogees.

Unfortunately, the delegates revived an unauthorized contract made with Crawford in 1885, which, at 10 percent, entitled him to more than $228,000. They also agreed to pay a note given to Major Perry Fuller, who acted as the Muscogees' attorney in 1866. Though the Muscogees had repudiated this debt, the note had passed to people who were influential in Washington. The noteholders agreed to accept $42,198, half the value of the note. After they were paid, only $10,000 remained for the tribe.

Enraged Muscogees held meetings, passed resolutions against their officials, and charged that Crawford had divided his fee with the delegates and other Muscogee leaders. An attempt was made to recover the money under a congressional law that required Department of Interior approval of attorneys' contracts with Indians. Trying to stop the attacks, Chief Legus C. Perryman called the Council on 19 June to petition the federal government for a per capita distribution of $400,000 accumulated under the treaty of 1866. Under a provision of this treaty, the $400,000 was a debt that would draw 5 percent interest until it could be paid per capita to the Muscogees. A resolution to censure the delegates for paying the Crawford fee passed in the House of Warriors but failed in the House of Kings. Although the Council did not approve a motion to impeach Perryman, it did adopt the resolution calling for the per capita distribution. Porter finally admitted that he had paid the money to others, rather than to Crawford (Debo 348–50). Particularly during the summer and fall 1889, the *Muskogee Daily Phoenix* was filled with reports, summaries of investigations, letters to the editor, and explanations from the accused on the misuse of per capita funds.

In the last third of the novel, Callahan shifts from discussing Muskogee history to describing the murder of Sitting Bull and the massacre of the Sioux, which corresponds to the events at Wounded Knee in 1890. Callahan's sudden shift from Muscogee to Lakota Sioux issues reflects current events and her tribe's earlier connection with the Lakota. In the midst of public fury over Custer's defeat in 1876, the commissioner of indian affairs tried to persuade the Sioux to settle among the Muscogee. Spotted Tail, American Horse, Red Dog, Not Afraid of His Horses, and other prominent Sioux chiefs arrived in late 1876 to meet with Muscogee leaders at a council held near Okmulgee. The Lakotas decided to remain on their own land (Debo 232–33; *Cherokee Advocate* (Tahlequah, Cherokee Nation) 21 october and 18 November 1876).

Chapter 18, "Turmoil with the Indians," introduces the issues of the starvation of the Sioux and the spread of the Ghost Dance during 1890. In 1889, the U.S. government reduced the beef issue at the Rosebud reservation by two million pounds, at Pine Ridge by one million, and at other agencies by proportional amounts. Further, Congress had cut the appropriation for subsistence and civilization to the Sioux for fiscal year 1890 to nine hundred thousand dollars, one hundred thousand less than the two previous years. Rations were cut accordingly, bringing hunger to the Sioux reservations during the winter of 1889–90. Things did not improve the next year. Because the House of Representatives did not pass the regular Indian Appropriation Act for fiscal year 1891 until August 1890, clothing and other annuity goods failed to reach the Sioux until the depths of winter (see Utley, *Last Days*).

The messianic Ghost Dance Religion, led by Wovoka (Jack Wilson, Paiute), spread across the Plains in the late 1880s and 1890. Wovoka predicted that the Plains would again support millions of buffalo and that whites would disappear. In October 1889, Lakota leader Kicking Bird brought news of the new religion to Sitting Bull at the Standing Rock reservation, South Dakota. The Hunkpapa chief allowed Kicking Bird to teach his people the Ghost Dance, although John McLaughlin, the tribe's agent, ordered police to escort the Ghost Dancer off the reservation. By mid-November, Ghost Dancing was so prevalent among the Sioux that most other activities ceased. White fears of the impact of the movement greatly increased. When Sitting Bull's name was listed as among the "fomenters," General Nelson A. Miles arranged for Buffalo Bill Cody to try to persuade the chief, who had been in Cody's Wild West Show during the 1885 season, to come to Chicago for a conference with Miles. McLaughlin managed to have this plan rescinded. Miles then ordered Lieutenant Colonel William F. Drum, commander of troops at Fort Yates, to "secure the person of Sitting Bull" (qtd. in Utley, *Last Days* 124, n.17). On 15 December 1890, forty-three Indian police surrounded Sitting Bull's cabin. Lieutenant Bull Head, the Indian policeman in charge, informed Sitting Bull that he was a prisoner and would be taken to the agency. When they emerged from the cabin, Ghost Dancers had gathered outside. As Bull Head and Sergeant Red Tomahawk tried to force Sitting Bull toward his horse, one of Sitting Bull's followers, Catch-the-Bear, fired a rifle at Bull Head, who fired as he fell. Trying to shoot his assailant, the policeman hit Sitting Bull in the chest. At the same time, Red Tomahawk shot Sitting Bull in the back of his head. Only the arrival of a cavalry detachment saved the Indian police from annihilation.

A group of fleeing Hunkpapas reached Big Foot's Miniconjou camp near the fork of Cherry Creek and the Cheyenne River, not far from the Cheyenne River agency in central South Dakota. The Miniconjous regarded Big Foot, called Spotted Elk when he rode with Sitting Bull against government troops, as one of the outstanding chiefs in their tribe's history because of his skill as a negotiator. Like Sitting Bull, Big Foot was committed to the old ways. He briefly embraced the Ghost Dance because of its promise to restore traditional Lakota life. On 17 December, the War Department issued orders for Big Foot's arrest as a troublemaker. As soon as the chief learned of Sitting Bull's death, he started his group of Ghost Dancers toward the Pine Ridge reservation in southern South Dakota, hoping for protection from the soldiers. The cavalry overtook them on 28 December. The next day, soldiers searched the angry warriors for guns. As the soldiers tried to grab a gun held by Black Coyote, whom Lakota eyewitnesses described as deaf or "crazy," a shot was fired (Utley, *Last Days* 212). The soldiers immediately and indiscriminately fired on the Miniconjous. When the Indians tried to flee, the soldiers raked the camp with big Hotchkiss guns placed on the hill. After the massacre ended, Big Foot and more than half of his people were dead or seriously wounded.

Through the debate between Carl Peterson and Wildfire over whether the Sioux should surrender, Callahan reveals her own mixed feelings about the events of that winter. Although Wildfire acknowledges that Carl is correct in arguing that resistance will have disastrous consequences for the Sioux, the fierce young leader replies that he and his young warriors would rather die than surrender: "is it right for the nation who have been trampled upon, whose land, whose property, whose liberty, whose everything but life, have been taken away, to meekly submit and still bow their heads for the yoke?" Inevitably, Wildfire, his wife, and his followers die in a battle, the details of which correspond to what happened at Wounded Knee. Through the stories of Chikena, a surviving widow, Callahan tells how the Sioux were starved by Indian agents and massacred by the army.[18] To show the range of contemporary opinions about the hostilities, Callahan both quotes from contemporary newspapers that supported the Indian cause and summarizes an article from the *St. Louis Republic* (16 December 1890) that commends the government on its slaughter and recommends that the dead bodies of the "savages" be used for fertilizer.[19] At one point, Callahan abandons speaking through her characters and addresses the reader directly. Although she acknowledges that a few army personnel were killed, Callahan sarcastically proclaims that it is not her province to "show how brave it was for a great, strong nation to quell a riot caused by the dancing of a few 'bucks'–for *civilized* soldiers to slaughter indiscriminately, Indian women and children. . . . Will history term the treatment of the Indians by the United States Government, right and honorable?" The novel closes with Carl's eloquent prayer for peace: "Let us pray, my brothers and sisters, that God will open the eyes of the Congress and people of the United States that they change their conduct toward the despised red race, and thus avert the evil sure to come upon us if they persist in their present treatment of the Indians." The hope for peaceful relations between Indians and non-Indians lies in the sensitivity of white characters such as Genevieve, Gerald Keithly, and Carl Peterson, who have learned to respect Native Americans and their culture and are committed to helping them adjust to the inevitable transition as non-Indians increasingly infringe on their land and traditions. At the end of the novel, Carl demonstrates his commitment to the welfare of the Lakota by bringing back three orphaned Sioux babies.[20] Callahan's strong emphasis on both Indians' and women's issues distinguishes her novel from other turn-of-the-century sentimental domestic romances written by non-Indian women. Callahan takes on the role of a "woman word warrior," creating "strong-hearted," intelligent heroines and sensitive heroes who educate her audience about Muscogee culture, Indians' and women's rights, and the mutual respect between the sexes essential to happy marriages. Though Callahan's *Wynema* lacks the polished style and seamless plot expected of experienced, sophisticated writers, it is nevertheless a moving and powerful call to action, which reveals the author's intelligence, knowlege of current issues, sensivity to native people, and commitment to justice. These qualities make *Wynema* a significant contribution to the history of Native American and women's literature.

NOTES

1. I found Callahan's *Wynema* after my *American Indian Literatures* was in press. Her name is listed on the title page of the novel as "S. Alice Callahan," but the *Indian Journal* (Eufaula, Creek Nation) and *Muskogee Daily Phoenix* refer to her as "Alice." The Library of Congress and the Oklahoma Historical Society each have a copy of *Wynema*, and the University of Illinois at Chicago has xerox copies.

The official name of the Creek Nation is now Muscogee (Creek) Nation. I have used *Muscogee* throughout to refer to the people and the nation, using *Creek* only where it was part of an official designation, such as the Creek regiment of the Confederate Army.

The title of the novel is probably derived from the name given to a Modoc woman who served as a liaison between the Modocs and U.S. government peace commissioners. Her real name was Toby Riddle, and she was a niece of Kintpuash (Captain Jack). During an 11 April 1873 meeting between the Modocs and the peace commissioners, Modoc leaders killed General Edward R. S. Canby. Commissioner Alfred B. Meacham was knocked unconscious by a ricocheting bullet. As Modocs were scalping and stripping Meacham, Toby Riddle frightened them away by crying that "the soldiers are coming!" She held Meacham's head in her lap until the soldiers arrived. The Modocs were subsequently removed to the Quapaw reservation in Indian Territory. Meacham gave Toby Riddle the name Winema, liberally interpreting it to mean "the Little Woman Chief." He recruited Toby, Frank Riddle, and some other Modocs to join his lecture tour, reenacting the attack and her heroic rescue. Meacham paid tribute to her in *Wi-ne-ma (the Woman Chief) and Her People* (1876) and in *Wigwam and War-Path; or the Royal Chief in Chains* (1875). Murray gives an objective account, especially on 49–51, 189–95, 311. See also Dorris.

In "S. Alice Callahan," Carolyn Thomas Foreman notes that the name was a favorite among the Indians and that the Muscogee journalist and writer Alexander Lawrence Posey (1873–1907) named his daughter Wynema (307, n.3). The idea for the title may also have been suggested by a Choctaw writer who signed her columns in the *Muskogee Daily Phoenix* as Wa-min-ne and Winema. Information provided by Daniel F. Littlefield Jr.

2. Samuel B. Callahan's Dawes Roll Number (1890) is 1535 (Cussetah Town, Creek Nation Roll, Card No. 464, Field No. 466, Dawes Census Cards, 1301, Roll 60). He and his children also appear on the 1890 Cussetah Tribal Town Census Roll (Roll 7 RA 1212, 1 December, National Archives, Southwest Region, Fort Worth, Texas). Copies of both rolls are in the Oklahoma Historical Society, Oklahoma City. Information about Samuel Benton Callahan's life has been taken primarily from "Samuel Benton Callahan," in *The History of the State of Oklahoma*, comp. Luther B. Hill et al., (Chicago: Lewis, 1909), 2:322; "Capt. Callahan Dies Here Today," *Muskogee*

Times-Democrat 17 February 1911, 1.7, 3.1–2; "To Be Buried in His Old Tattered Uniform of Gray. Captain S. B. Callahan Loyal to His Colors in Death," *Muskogee Daily Phoenix* 18 February 1911, 1.7, 8.5; "Appendix, Samuel Benton Callahan." See also "Okmulgee News," *Indian Journal* 16 July 1885, 4.2, and 5 November 1885, 4.3.

S. B. Callahan and S. E. McAllester were married on 10 July 1858 in Hopkins County, Texas (copy of marriage certificate provided by Opal Lee Brinlee, Deputy County Clerk, Hopkins County). See also "Marriage Records of Hopkins County, Texas, 1846–1880," comp. Frances T. Ingmire (St. Louis: author, 1979). "Appendix, Samuel Benton Callahan" gives their marriage date as 1857 and says she was a daughter of the Reverend William Thornberg, a Methodist minister in Sulphur Springs (314). This information was undoubtedly taken from "Samuel Benton Callahan," in Hill et al., 2:322. "Death of Mrs. Callahan" (*Muskogee Daily Phoenix* 15 October 1891, 5.2) gives Sarah's birth date as 1839; she died in October 1891. In a letter to Carolyn Thomas Foreman dated 16 July 1955, Leila S. Howard, a granddaughter, said that Sarah Callahan's maiden name was Roundtree (Grant Foreman Collection, Box 3, Oklahoma Historical Society, Oklahoma City OK).

The names of the Callahan children are variously given. The 1880 census for Hopkins County lists Josie (21), J[ames] O (19), Eva (17), Benton [Samuel Benton, called "Benton"] (15), Alice (12), Gilis (11), Mortimer (7), and Blackburn (age not clear) (*1880 Census, Hopkins County, Texas*, comp. Frat E. Davis Hopkins County TX: Genealogical Society, 1988). I am grateful to Frat E. Davis for providing this information. The 1890 Cussetah Tribal Town Census Roll lists the children as Benton (Samuel Benton), Eva, Alice, Gipsie, Kenzie, and Edwin. Gilis and Gipsie are probably the same person. Evelyn, Dawes Roll No. 1536, is probably the Eva who appears on the earlier census lists (Creek Nation Roll, Card 464, Field 466). Kenzie appears as Walter K., Dawes Roll No. 1538 (Card 465, Field 467). James O.'s

Dawes Roll No. is 1425 (Card 433, Field 435). See Dawes Census Cards, 1301, Roll 60, Oklahoma Historical Society.

3. Biographical information about Alice Callahan has been taken from Reverend M. L. Butler, "In Memoriam [Alice Callahan]," *Our Brother in Red* (Muskogee, Creek Nation) 13 (11 January 1894):1. 2–3, and from Foreman, "S. Alice Callahan." Butler was the pastor at Harrell International Institute.

4. An 1876 description of the Wesleyan Female Institute's curriculum included courses on orthography; English grammar, composition, and rhetoric; history of the United States, England, Rome, France, and Greece; arithmetic and algebra; philosophy and moral philosophy; intermediate and senior French, German, and Latin; chemistry; and instrumental music, vocal music, drawing, and oil painting. Founded in 1846, the school went bankrupt and its buildings and lands were sold in 1900. See Hamrick; Brown 25, 48–49. Copies provided by Catharine Bushman, Staunton, Virginia, and Susan M. Clark, Reference Department, Staunton Public Library.

5. Harrell International Institute was named after the Reverend John Harrell, a famous Methodist missionary. For a history of the school, see Foreman, *Muskogee* 52–54. Copies of the Harrell catalog for 1890–91 and 1894 and of *The Harrell Monthly* are in the Alice M. Robertson Collection, Oklahoma Historical Society. Lauren Stuart Muller kindly gave me copies of these.

6. "Death of Mrs. Callahan" 5.2.

7. Butler, "In Memoriam" 1.2.

8. *Our Brother in Red* 13 (9 November 1893):1.5; Foreman 312, n.12.

9. *Our Brother in Red* reported on 21 December 1893 that she had been very much indisposed for several days (4.1). See also letters from Lulu Todd to Rubie Fears, 7 and 13 January 1894, typescripts by Carolyn Thomas Foreman, in Grant Foreman Collection, Box 3, Oklahoma Historical Society.

10. Bahktin calls this *heteroglossia* (324).

11. Ceremonial names such as Harjo, Fixico, and Emarthla, which Callahan uses in the novel, became family surnames. Several unrelated families took the name Harjo. Alexander Posey's maternal grandfather was Pahosa Harjo from Tuskegee. Chitto Harjo (Crazy Snake), who led the Muscogee opposition to allotment of tribal lands, came from another family. Information provided by Alan Cook, historic preservation officer, Muscogee (Creek) Nation; Daniel F. Littlefield Jr.; Debo 293–94.

12. Showalter indicates that novels by British women follow a similar pattern (28–29). Weir points out that following the Civil War, male and female novelists fashioned heroines who lacked the beauty, gentility, and decorous behavior associated with the sentimental heroine. They permitted their heroines to feel sexual stirrings and to reject marriage (193–95). See also Banta. In depicting Genevieve's adjustment to life in the Muscogee Nation, Callahan does not emphasize her heroine Genevieve's response to an unfamiliar, hostile landscape, as did many other nineteenth-century women authors of frontier novels. The heroines of other novels by women often labored to create gardens that reminded them of the homes they had left. See Kolodny 8–9.

13. Teaching was one of the few acceptable occupations open to unmarried women on the frontier. Griswold 20.

14. Not until 1920 did women achieve the right to vote in national elections. For histories of women's rights movements in the United States, see Flexner.

15. Callahan, "Teacher's Report," 6 September–15 November 1892, 1 February–14 March 1893, and 15 March–20 May 1893, Wealaka Mission, School Department, Muskogee Nation, Creek Schools, Tullahassee Mission, POS, Box No. CRN 47, No. 37071, Oklahoma Historical Society. She had between fifty-six and fifty-nine students each quarter.

16. The name of the war derives from Tecumseh's magic Red Stick, which would point out the direction of his enemies and overcome

them and which he used when he taught the Muscogees his "Dance of the Lakes." Debo 76.

17. Chitto Harjo was captured and imprisoned in January 1901. Gibson 502–4.

18. Beatrice Medicine (Lakota Sioux) indicates that the name "Chikena" is made-up. It has no meaning in Lakota.

19. On 16 December 1990, the newspaper was equally vicious about the death of Sitting Bull: "Sitting Bull has been regarded by his people as an Indian patriot. He is now merely a good Indian" (6.3). In an editorial on his death published the next day, the paper described him as "a greasy savage, who rarely bathed, and was liable at any time to become infected with vermin. During the whole of his life he entertained the remarkable delusion that he was a free-born American with some rights in the country of his ancestors." His death removed "one of the last obstacles in the path of progress. He will now make excellent manure of the crops, which will grow over him when his reservation is civilized" (6.2).

20. Although the adoption of these infant survivors by "Christian" families was widely hailed at the time, such enthusiastic responses by non-Indians ignored the long-term cultural consequences to the babies. See Flood, *Lost Bird of Wounded Knee*, which chronicles the sad life of one such survivor.

WYNEMA

behind the great mountain, and points them to the circuitous trail over its side which he tells them has been made by the great warriors of their tribe as they went to the "happy hunting-ground."

Sixteen miles above this village of tepees stood another and a larger town in which was a mission-school, superintended by Gerald Keithly, a missionary sent by the Methodist assembly to promote civilization and christianity among these lowly people. Tall, young and fair, of quiet, gentle manners, and possessing a kindly sympathy in face and voice, he easily won the hearts of his dark companions. The "Mission" was a small log-house, built in the most primitive style, but it accommodated the small number of students who attended school; for the Indians long left to follow after pleasure are loth to quit her shrine for the nobler one of Education. It was hard to impress upon them, young or old, the necessity of becoming educated. If their youths handled the bow and rifle well and were able to endure the greatest hardships, unmurmuringly, their education was complete; hence every device within the ken of an ingenious mind, calculated to amuse and attract the attention of the little savages, and to cause them to desire to remain near the school-room, was summoned to the aid of this teacher, "born not made." He mingled with the Indians in their sports whenever practicable, and endeavored in every way to show them he had come to help and not to hinder them. Nor did he confine himself to the village in which his work lay, for he felt the command "Go ye into *all* the world and preach the gospel to *every* creature," impelling him onward. The village of tepees, Wynema's home, knew him and welcomed him; in the abode of her father he was an honored guest, where, with a crowd gathered about him, he hold of the love and mercy of a Savior, of the home that awaits the faithful, and urged his dusky brethren to educate their children in the better ways of their pale-faced friends. At first he talked through an interpreter, but feeling the greater influence he would gain by speaking to the Indians in their own tongue, he mastered their language and dispensed with the interpreter. But to Wynema he always spoke the mother tongue—English; for, he reasoned, she is young and can readily acquire a new language, and it will profit her to know the English. His was the touch that brought into life the slumbering ambition for knowledge and for a higher life, in the breast of the little Indian girl. Her father and mother carried her to the "Mission" to hear Gerald Keithly preach, and missing her when they started off the following day, they found her in the school-room, standing near her friend, listening eagerly and attentively to all he said and wonder-struck at the recitations of the pupils, simple though they were.

"Father," she said, "let me stay here and listen always; I want to know all this the pupils are talking about." "No, my child," answered her father, "your mother and I could not get along without you; we can build you a school at home, and you may stay there and listen."

"When, father, when?" Wynema asked eagerly. "Ask Gerald Keithly when he comes," he answered, to divert her attention from himself. Then the days became weeks to Wynema, impatiently awaiting the coming of her friend.

Every day she thought with delight of the school her father would build, and every day planned it all for the benefit of her little friends and playmates, who had become anxious also, from hearing Wynema's description of school life, to enter "learning's hall." When Gerald Keithly finally came, he found a small school organized under Wynema, waiting for a house and teacher.

"Do you really wish to go to school so much, little girl?" he asked Wynema, only to see her cheeks flush and her eyes flash with desire.

"Oh, so much!" clasping her hands; "may I?" she asked.

"If your father wishes," Gerald answered gladly.

"Father said ask you, and now you say, if father wishes," she began disappointedly.

"Well, then, you may, for I shall send off for you a teacher, right away. Now, then, go tell your playmates;" and he patted her cheek.

"Oh, I am so glad!" and she looked at him, her eyes full of grateful tears; then ran gleefully away.

Gerald Keithly then went to the father, stalwart Choe Harjo, and asked:

"Do you want a school here? and will you build a house? If so, I will send and get you a teacher."

"Yes," he answered, "the child wishes it; so be it."

"Would you like a man or woman for teacher?" Gerald questions.

"Let it be a woman, and she may live with us; I want the child to be with her always, for she is so anxious to learn. We will do all we can for the teacher, if she will live among us."

"I am sure of that," answered Gerald, warmly pressing the Indian's hand.

So the cry rang out in the great Methodist assembly; "A woman to teach among the Indians in the territory. Who will go?" and it was answered by one from the sunny Southland—a young lady, intelligent and pretty, endowed with the graces of heart and head, and surrounded by the luxuries of a Southern home. Tenderly reared by a loving mother, for her father had long ago gone to rest, and greatly loved by her brother and sisters of whom she was the eldest, she was physically unfit to bear the hardships of a life among the Indians; but God had endowed her with great moral courage and endurance, and she felt the call to go too strenuously, to allow any obstacles to obstruct her path.

She understood the responsibility of the step she was about to take, but, as she said to her mother who was endeavoring to persuade her to change her resolve, and pleading tearfully to keep her daughter with her:

"God has called me and I dare not refuse to do his bidding. He will take care of me among the Indians as he cares for me here; and he will take care of you while I am gone and bring me back to you again. Never fear, mother, dear, our Father takes care of his obedient, believing children, and will not allow any harm to befall them."

Thus came civilization among the Tepee Indians.

2

The School

Genevieve Weir stood at her desk in the Indian school-house, reflecting: How shall I make them understand that it is God's word that I am reading and God to whom I am talking? She deliberated earnestly. What do they know about the Supreme Being?

Poor little girl! She made the common mistake of believing she was the only witness for God in that place. Wynema often spoke of Gerald Keithly in her broken way; but Genevieve believed him to be miles away.

"I shall begin the exercises with the reading of the Word, and prayer, at any rate, and perhaps they will understand by my expression and attitude," she determined at length, calling the school to order. She read a portion of the fourteenth chapter of St. John — that sweet, comforting gospel — then clasping her hands and raising her eyes, she uttered a simple prayer to the "all-Father," asking that he open the hearts of the children, that they might be enabled to understand His word; and that He give her such great love for her dusky pupils, that her only desire be in dividing this Word among them. The pupils understood no word of it, but the tone went straight to each one's heart and found lodgment there. At recess Wynema came and stood by her teacher's side with deep wonder in her great, black eyes.

"Mihia," (teacher) she asked, "you talk to God?" and she clasped her hands and raised her eyes, imitating Genevieve's attitude.

"Yes, dear," Genevieve answered, delightedly surprised at the acute understanding of the child. "God is our good Father who lives in heaven, up there," pointing upward, "and is all around us now and all the time. Do you know anything about God, dear?"

"Gerald Keithly talk to God when he come here," the child answered simply.

"Does he come here often?" questioned the teacher next.

"Yes, sometime. But, Mihia," returning to the subject nearest her heart, "you 'fraid God?"

"Why, no, Wynema," she replied putting her hand on the child's shoulder; "why should I be afraid of the all-Father who loves me so? Are you afraid of your father and mother?"

"O, no; but when I am bad girl, I feel sorry and go off to left them," she said soberly.

"Why do you wish to leave them then? Do you go off when you are a good girl?" Genevieve asked.

"Not when I am good girl, when I am bad. Then my ma and pa ought whip me, but they don't," the child replied.

"Well, dear, God loves you more than your father and mother can possibly love you; yes, He loves you when you are bad, and when you are good. Sometimes, when you are bad, He will punish you, but He will love you always. Don't be afraid of God, little one, but try to love Him and be a good girl,"—with that she stooped and kissed the child, who ran and told her playmates all the words of her teacher.

After this the children seemed to listen to the morning services more seriously and attentively, and before many weeks elapsed were able to join with their teacher in repeating a prayer she taught them.

To many persons the difficulty of teaching our language to any foreigner seems almost insurmountable; and teaching the Indians seems especially difficult. Thus Genevieve Weir's faraway friends thought, and many were the inquiries she received concerning her work.

"How did she make them understand her, and how could she understand them? How could she teach them when they could not understand a word she said? Wasn't she afraid to live among those dark savages?" etc., etc. To all of which she gave characteristic replies.

"God made the Indians as he made the Caucasian—from the same mold. He loves the work of His hands and for His sake I love these 'dark savages,' and am, therefore, not in the least afraid of them. They know that I have come to live among them for their good, and they try to show their gratitude by being as kind to me as they know how. I talk to the older ones mostly by signs, but the children have gotten so they can understand me when I speak to them. Sometimes it is rather difficult to make the people at home, at Choe Harjo's, understand me, when Wynema is not by to interpret for me. For instance: yesterday I wanted an egg. I spoke the word egg, slowly several times, but the Indians shook their heads and said something in their language which as greatly puzzled me. Then taking some straw I made a nest and put some feathers in it; you have no idea how quickly they grasped my meaning, and laughing at my device, brought what I had asked for. Then taking the egg, I held it up before them, pronouncing the word egg, slowly, which they all repeated after me. You may be sure they always understand what I want when I call for an egg now. It is remarkable what bright minds these 'untaught savages' have. I know you would be surprised at the rapid progress my pupils make, notwithstanding their great drawback of being ignorant of our own language.

"My little Wynema, of whom I have spoken before, has only to hear a word and she has it. She learns English very rapidly and can understand almost anything I say; and she is a great help to me, as she often interprets for me at home and at school.

"It would be rather amusing and interesting to my friends to come into my school-room when I am hearing the language lesson. It taxes my ingenuity to the uttermost, sometimes, to accurately convey my meaning and make myself understood. I have no advanced classes, yet, but I intend to teach the ancient and modern languages and higher mathematics before I quit this people—you see I do not intend leaving *soon*, and I will never leave them from fear or dislike."

3

Some Indian Dishes

"What have you there, Wynema?" asked Genevieve Weir of her pupil one evening as she stepped into the "cook-room" and found Wynema eagerly devouring a round, dark-looking mass, which she was taking from a corn-shuck. All around the wide fire-place sat Indian women engaged in the same occupation, all eating with evident relish.

"Oh, Mihia! It is blue dumpling. I luf it. Do you luf it?" she asked offering the shuck to Genevieve.

"I do not know what it is. I never saw any before. How is it made?" she made answer.

"It is meal beat from corn, beat fine, and it is beans with the meal. Shell the beans an' burn the shells of it, an' put it in the meal, an' put the beans in an' wet it an' put it in a shuck, an' tie the shuck so tight it won't spill out an' put it in the water an' boil it," the child replied, out of breath with her long and not very lucid explanation.

"What makes the dumpling so dark?" asked the teacher, eying the mass which she held in her hand, rather curiously.

"That is the burn shells; we burn it an' put in the meal an' it makes it blue. Goot! eat some, Mihia. It is so goot."

Miss Weir took a small morsel of the dumpling in her mouth, for she was not prepossessed with its looks, and ate it with difficulty for it was tough and tasteless.

"No I don't want any; thank you, dear, I think I don't like it very well because I never ate any; I should have to practice a long time before I could eat blue dumpling very well;" and she smiled away the frown on the child's brow.

Soon after this, supper was announced and the family gathered around a table, filled with Indian dainties.

There in the center of the table, stood the large wooden bowl of sofke, out of which each one helped himself or herself, eating with a wooden spoon, and lifting the sofke from the bowl directly to the mouth. This dish, which is made of the hardest flint corn, beaten or chopped into bits, and boiled until quite done in water containing a certain amount of lye, is rather palatable when fresh, but as is remarkable, the Indians, as a general thing, prefer it after it has soured and smells more like a swill-barrel than anything else. Besides the sofke, were soaked corn bread, which is both sour and heavy; dried venison; a soup with an unspellable name, made of corn and dried beef, which is really the most palatable of all the Indian dishes; and opuske, a drink composed of meal made from green corn roasted until perfectly dry and brown, and beaten in a stone mortar until quite fine; mixed with water.

Not a very inviting feast for Genevieve Weir, or indeed, for any person unaccustomed to such fare; but that the Indians, surrounding the board considered it such, was evident by the dispatch with which they ate.

And it is strange that, though always accustomed to such fare, the Indians are not a dyspeptic people. We of this age are constantly talking and thinking of ways and means by which to improve our cookery to suit poor digestive organs. How we would hold up our hands in horror at the idea of placing blue dumplings on our tables! And yet, we are a much more dyspeptic people than the "blue dumpling" eaters, struggle though we do to ward off the troublesome disease.

"Mihia, the sun is far up. We must go to school. You no get up?" Wynema coming into her teacher's bedroom late one morning. She had waited for Miss Weir to make her appearance at the breakfast-table, and, as she did not do so, went in search of her. There she lay tossing and moaning, with a raging fever, but still conscious. The child, who was unaccustomed to illness in any form, stood looking at her in surprise.

"Come here, dear," said Genevieve, calling her to the bed. "Tell your mamma I am sick, and cannot teach to-day. Your father will please go to the school-house and tell the children. I hope I shall be all right by to-morrow, but I cannot stand on my feet to-day."

Wynema ran to tell her mother, who soon came into the sick-room.

"Seek?" questioned the mother. "What eat?"

"Yes; I do not care for anything to eat," Miss Weir replied; thinking, "Oh, I shall starve to death here if I am sick long!"

"Send for medicine man, he cure you quick," the woman urged.

Wynema then spoke up; "Medicine man make you well, Mihia, get him come. He make Luce well when she sick."

"Well, send for him then, please; for I do want to get well right away," she smiled feebly.

The "medicine man" came in directly and looking at the patient closely, took his position in the corner, where with a bowl of water, a few herbs and a small cane, he concocted his "cure alls." Genevieve watched him curiously and with good reason, for a more queerly dressed person or a more curious performance, it would have been hard to find. With his leggins, his loose, fringed, many-colored hunting-shirt, his beaded moccasins, his long, colored blanket sweeping the ground, and his head-dress with the fringe touching his eyebrows, he was both picturesque and weird. His performance consisted of blowing through a cane into the water in which he had mixed the herbs, and going through with an incantation in a low, indistinct tone. What the words were could not be told by any of the Indians—except the medicine man—but all of them had great faith in this personage and held him rather in awe.

After the blowing had been going on for some time and the incantation repeated and re-repeated the medicine was offered to the patient, who made a pretense of taking it.

"Tell him I am better now, Wynema, and he may go," she said to the child who was taking the performance in.

After that dignitary, the "medicine man," had retired, Genevieve used the few simple remedies at hand, known to herself, and to her joy and surprise, was able to resume her school duties on the following day.

The "medicine man" was never called in to wait upon Miss Weir again.

4

The Busk

"Oh, Mihia, we all go to busk!" cried Wynema bounding toward her teacher one evening, some weeks after the events recorded in the foregoing chapter.

"You go. Everybody go an' you have no school, we go an' dance, dance," she said jumping in glee.

"When are you going?" asked her teacher smiling at her joy. "I heard Sam Fixico and Hoseka talking about the busk to-day, but I did not know we were to go so soon."

"We go to-night. Get there soon in morning, an' women cook all day an' dance at night an' eat all next day. Have goot time!" and she clapped her hands merrily, slipping by her teacher's side.

When the two reached home they found everybody busily making preparations for the approaching festivities. Wynema's mother, and the fair Kineno met them and explained to "Mihia."

"We go busk 'night. Eferypoty, no school, you go—nopoty stay with you—all go busk."

"Very well, I shall go to the busk, too; I have never been to one and I think I shall like it. Let me help you to get ready;" and they worked with a will until all things were prepared.

At sundown they started for the camping-ground which was some miles distant—how many could not be exactly told for an Indian never measures distance—and reached there in time to refresh themselves by a good sleep, before the early dawn roused them from their slumbers. By the increasing light Genevieve could distinguish what seemed to her numberless rows of tents, placed in something of a semi-circle about an open space, which was bounded on its other side by groves and clumps of trees.

After breakfast, the men gathered together talking and smoking; the women went busily to work preparing for the morrow's feast, and Genevieve, left to herself, looked about her for something of interest, which she finally found.

To the right of the plain was a small grove of trees, some distance from the tents. In the grove stood an old man whom Genevieve readily recognized as the "medicine man," not only from his looks, but there he was, going through his incantations and blowing through his cane, which had grown longer, into a kettle. As she stood looking on, amused at the M. D.'s proceedings, a voice at her elbow startled her.

"You seem at a loss to know what all this ceremony means," said the voice.

Genevieve turned and beheld a tall, fair, young, American gentleman, with a laughing light in his blue-gray eyes.

"Pardon me," he continued, "I did not mean to startle you; I should not have addressed you, but you seemed so amazed and wonder-struck, I determined to enlighten you concerning what you shall have to expect. Shall I go on?"

"Oh, yes, pray do!" she smiled upon him. "But first tell me—you are the long-expected Mr. Keithly?"

"Yes, and you are the well-beloved Miss Weir; for you haven't any idea how much these Indians think of you. I have an apology and explanation to make to you, for not coming to see you before. Now I don't want you to think meanly of me, Miss Weir," he said, looking down into her brown, upturned eyes; "but the reason I did not meet you as I should have done and as I wished to do, is that I wanted to see first whether you would stay after you came. I wanted you to try your own strength and faith and endurance by being all alone among a strange people, before I made my appearance. If you had not done well I should never have come here to meet you as I have. Did I do wrong?"

"I don't believe you can realize how hard it was sometimes, and how very near I have been to giving it up," she said in a low tone; "your presence occasionally would have been encouraging; but it is all over now, and I'll forgive you if you'll promise never to be guilty of the same offense."

"Oh, you may be sure I'll promise that. It will be no hardship, I assure you, for white people, and young ladies especially, are rare in these parts. We can be a mutual pleasure and benefit if we will; if I can do anything at all for you now or at any time, let me know and I shall take pleasure in serving you," he said with a smile and bow.

"Thank you, and ditto," she smiled sweetly. "And now tell me what I shall have to expect, as you began."

"Well, in the first place, do you recognize that very queerly dressed personage in the grove yonder? Perhaps you have seen him before this?" he asked.

"Oh, yes, I am very well acquainted with him. He is the 'medicine man.' Then she related what the reader already knows concerning the visit of the M. D.

"It is strange what implicit confidence these Indians have in their 'medicine man,' and in what awe they hold his strange ceremonies," she said, watching the performance of the 'medicine man,' with the least expression of contempt in her soft, brown eyes.

Gerald Keithly looked at her quietly.

"Do you have any faith in our physicians, Miss Weir?" he asked.

"Yes, indeed, I always want a physician when I am ill," Genevieve answered in surprise.

"Which is quite natural," he said quietly. "Every people, no matter how ignorant or savage, has its physician, and the M. D. of every race has his peculiar modus operandi.

"If one of our physicians should come into the sick-room of our savage friends here, and begin to feel the patient's pulse and prescribe, by examining the tongue, these people would be as much surprised at his operations as you were at this M. D.'s. The 'medicine man' is compounding a supply of health-preservative to last through the year. You see the men are crowding around him in answer to the signal he made just now. They will all partake of the beverage in the kettle, which is a mixture of all the herbs known to these people, and this will be their year's supply of physic. You will think they are going to die, for a while; but they will lie around and rest to-day and be ready for the feast to-morrow."

"Why do not the women drink of the stuff, also? It seems to me they should need to be well if any one does, for they do the greater part of the work," the little skeptic next asked.

"So they do; but they would not be able to prepare the viands for the feast to-morrow if they should partake; so they desist for their husbands' sake, and take medicine when they need it, which they rarely do, as they are a healthy people."

"Why is this gathering called a busk? I have wanted to ask this question ever since I heard the word, but could find no one to explain so that I could understand," said Genevieve.

"Because of the time of the year when it is held, after the coming of green corn or roasting ears. The Indians eat no green corn until after they have had a busk, when they have cleansed their system and prepared themselves for a bountiful feast of it. The dance which they will hold to-night is a thank-offering to the bountiful Supplier who has made their corn crop to flourish. Now, I think you understand what you shall have to expect. It is first a feast, lasting through the day; second, a dance to-night; and last but best, a feast to-morrow. I hope you can survive through the day, and you will be all right to-morrow," he added laughing. "If you dwell among the Romans, you must abide by their laws and follow their customs whenever practicable."

"And whenever right," she added, seriously.

5

The Dance

Wynema crept up to her teacher as she stood talking with Gerald Keithly, and looked at them both, wonderingly. The child had been playing with her little friends and now came in search of the one whom she liked best.

"Wynema, little girl, don't you know me?" asked Gerald Keithly bending over to look in her face; "I have been telling Mihia how you all like her; was I right?" and he placed his hand under her chin.

"'Mihia' knows I luf her," the child answered drawing herself away from him and looking up confidingly into her teacher's face.

"But why do you love her," he persisted. "She is a pale-face. Do you think she loves you?"

"Oh, yes, I know she does," answered Wynema, caressing her teacher's hand, "and I luf her, for she is so good."

"You have grown wise as well as tall, my little lady. Now, may I present your royal highness with this?" and he bowed low before the child, holding up a paper bag. "Tell me now, do you love me too?"

Wynema glanced up at her teacher, her eyes questioning mischievously, "Shall I?" to which silent interrogative Miss Weir nodded assent.

Then the little maid replied:

"I *like* you; I *luf* 'Mihia.' "

"Thank you, my little lady for so deep a regard," replied Keithly, bowing with his hand on his heart. "I don't think I can give this to you, now, since you care so little for me," and he held up the sack tantalizingly; Wynema turned away proudly disappointed, but deigned not to reply.

"There, you may have it," Keithly called after her. "I will not tease you any more."

Wynema looked up at her teacher with tears in her eyes.

"Take it, dear," Genevieve said, and the child took the candy, murmuring her thanks in a low tone.

"You have robbed her gratitude of its sweetness; she thanks you only in words," Miss Weir said.

"Yes, I should not tease her so; but I can hardly refrain from doing so, I am naturally such a tease, and she is so sweet and pretty. Forgive me, little one; and let us now go to the dance."

Wynema led the way, smiling and happy as ever. The three soon reached the grass-grown plain where the Indian men and women had already collected. In the middle of the plain sat the medicine man, who seemed to be master of ceremonies, and all around him, in single file, danced first the men then the women. Danced? Well, not as you understand the word, my reader, but in a kind of a hop, up and down—a motion not in the least graceful or rhythmic, but it was in accordance with the music. The medicine man directed all the motions and figures by the tune he sang. He droned one tune and the company started; another and they stopped. And what music, or rather queer noises this savage musician made! No Chinese love-song could have compared with it. His voice was accompanied by the jingling and clanking of shot and shells, bound on the ankles of the dancers. What a strange, weird scene it all was for this girl unaccustomed to such sights! She looked at it with amaze; the plain, with its semi-circle border of tents; the gaudily and fantastically dressed dancers; the medicine man with his strange ceremonies; and above and beyond all, the clanking of the shells and shot, mixed with the groaning and grunting of the musician tended more to strike with terror than admiration. Gerald Keithly laughed at his companion's look of consternation.

"How long will this last?" she asked.

"Oh, four or five hours—only a short time; you don't mean to convey the idea that you are tired already? You would not make much of an Indian, would you?" he asked teasingly.

"No, I am afraid not, if this constitutes one. Can I not retire to my tent? Will I offend them?" she asked, looking anxiously toward the dancers.

"Oh, no, they are too busily engaged to notice your disappearance. I will escort you if you will allow me,"—and he walked by her side.

As they walked back toward her tent, Miss Weir exclaimed vehemently: "Oh, that the Indians would quit these barbaric customs! Why is it they will cling to them no matter how much they associate with white people?" Gerald spoke quietly and courteously, "Do you think, Miss Weir, that if our Indian brother yonder, now full of the enjoyment of the hour, could step into a ball-room, say in Mobile, with its lights and flowers, its gaudily, and if you will allow it, indecently dressed dancers—do you think he would consider us more civilized than he? Of course that is because he is an uncouth savage," with a slight tinge of irony. "Now, I am going to be ignorant and uncouth enough to agree with him in some things. In the first place, he is more sensible in the *place* he chooses. The Indians select an open space, in the fresh, pure air, in preference to a tight, heated room—an evidence of their savagery. In the second place, the squaws always buy enough cloth to make a full dress, even if it be red calico. You may go among them so long and often as you choose, and you will never find a low-necked, short-sleeved dress—which is another evidence of their ignorance. In the third place, they are more moderate in their dancing. A few nights during the year are sufficient for the untaught savage to indulge in the 'light fantastic,' whereas, every night in the week, during 'the season,' hardly suffices for the Caucasian. In the—"

"There; that will do," laughingly remonstrated Genevieve; "I am fully convinced of the superiority of our red brothers, Mr. Champion; I shall never make use of such remarks again. It is truly a pity the Indian has not more champions such as you, Mr. Keithly; for then they would not be so grossly misrepresented as they now are."

There was a ring of sincerity in Genevieve's voice that won her young companion's heart and made him more her friend than ever. They parted at the door of her tent, as the hour was late, and were long wrapped in the arms of slumber, when the dancers desisted for the night.

Next day dawned bright and sunshiny and was spent in feasting, after which the Indians smoked the "pipe of peace," and returned to their several homes.

Gerald Keithly bade Genevieve "au revoir" as he said the grass should not grow high between them. That he was a great favorite among the Indians could plainly be seen by the hearty welcome, and cordial hand-shake each gave him on his departure; and as for Genevieve, she thought how pleasant it was to have so companionable a person near. And Gerald—

"Ah, well for us all some sweet hope lies,
Deeply buried from human eyes!"

6

An Indian Burial

Years passed on with the same round of school duties for Genevieve Weir—duties crowned with joy and pride, as she watched the gradual unfolding of mind and soul to the touch of her magic wand—the influence of love opening doors that giant force could not set the least ajar. Wynema continued to be her greatest joy and pride and was more than ever her *vade mecum*, of whom she wrote often to her home friends.

"She learns faster and retains more of what she learns, than any child of whatever hue it has been my fortune to know. She is a constant reader and greets a new book with the warmth of a friend. I have directed her course of reading, and I venture to say, there is not a child in Mobile or anywhere else who has read less spurious matter than she. It is amusing to see her curl up over Dickens or Scott, and grow animated over Shakespeare, whose plays she lives out; and it is interesting to watch the different emotions, in sympathy with the various characters, chase each other over her face. Of the good ones she will say, "This is you, Mihia, but you are better." Dear child; would that I were as perfect as she believes me to be!

One evening as Miss Weir and her pupil were returning from school, they heard strange sounds—such as groaning, wailing, lamenting and sobbing—proceeding from a cabin not far from the roadside; and Miss Weir turned to Wynema for explanation.

"Some one must be dead, and they are singing the death-chant," said Wynema. "Mamma said Sam Emarthla was very sick—so I suppose—so I suppose it is that he is dead." She always spoke brokenly when she was touched. "Shall it be that we may go and look upon the dead?"

"Yes, dear," responded her teacher; "and it may be that we can speak a comforting word to the bereft ones. But tell me before we go in, what is the meaning of the death-chant."

"The death-chant? How can I tell you, Mihia? It begins by telling the good deeds of the dead person; of his virtues; what a good hunter he was; how brave he always was; and ends by carrying him over the mountain side to the happy hunting-ground, there to live forever, among dogs and horses, with bows and arrows and game of all kinds in abundance."

By the time she finished speaking they had reached the cabin door, and on looking in, they beheld the room full of sympathizing friends, who pushed aside and made an entrance for the new-comers.

Going up to the bed where the corpse lay dressed and decorated for burial, Genevieve found the stricken wife lying face downward on the breast of her dead husband. Not a sound escaped her lips, for she seemed stunned by her grief. Here was no fashionable grief with its dress of sable hue, its hangings of crepe, and stationery with its inch-wide band of black, such as Madison-Square widows use. Ah! no, here was real, simple, heart-felt grief such as the ignorant and uneducated feel; grief such as Eve felt over the death of her well-beloved son.

Ranged around the bed were the mourners, noisy at first, but now awed into silence by the presence of a real grief. In a corner of the room Genevieve noticed the medicine man, going through with his incantations as usual, in a very subdued voice. Genevieve motioned to Wynema who stood apart looking reverently on, and the girl came and stood by her teacher's side.

"Tell Chineka for me," Miss Weir said, "that God, the good Father above, knows her grief and will help her to bear it if she will ask Him; that He has only taken Emarthla for a while, when she can go and join him and live forever above." All this and more Miss Weir spoke and Wynema interpreted to the sorrowing wife, who only glanced up gratefully at the teacher's face.

After asking a few questions relative to the burial, and finding that all things had been prepared for interment the following day, Genevieve and Wynema departed from the bereaved home.

Early in the forenoon of the following day Choe Harjo, his family and Genevieve, repaired to the burial-ground where they found quite a number of the friends and relatives of the deceased man. In a few moments, strong pall-bearers carrying the corpse which was placed in a rude wooden box, appeared, followed by the widow and the nearest of kin. Arriving at the grave, the box would have been immediately lowered, had not a friendly hand stopped the pall-bearers, and a voice said something which caused them to put the coffin down and stand with uncovered heads. Looking up in surprise, Genevieve beheld Gerald Keithly with bible in hand, proceeding in reverent way to conduct the burial services. The Indians listened to him with fixed attention, and when, as he finished reading, he spoke a few words in their own language concerning the dead, words of praise for his good deeds, and words of sympathy for the sorrowing wife and loved ones, the tears ran softly down the cheeks of many, and a moisture gathered in the eyes of Chineka who, for the first time since her bereavement, showed signs of being conscious of her surroundings.

When the service was over, after the prayer had been offered and the hymn sung, friends of the dead man placed inside the grave beside the coffin, his gun and ammunition, bows and arrows, and a sufficient amount of provision to carry him on his journey to the happy hunting-ground.

Then the coffin was well sprinkled with rice, and the company disbanded and went home.

It would be well to say here what should have been said before; in preparing a man for burial, the Indians dress him in full hunting-suit, boots, and hat. Near him in the coffin, lies his pipe and tobacco, so that when he is ready to start to his final home, he has all things at hand to cheer and comfort him.

7

A Strange Ceremony

"Why do the Indians go by the creek on their way home?" asked Miss Weir of Gerald Keithly as he rode by her side on the way home from the burial.

"Wait and you will see," he answered briefly.

When the Indians reached the creek they all dismounted and walked into the water, some of them bathing themselves and some only throwing the water on their heads and faces; after which procedure they walked out of the water backward and turned homewards.

"Mihia, you don't drive away disease or illness—throw the water over yourself," and Wynema sprinkled herself generously. Genevieve looked toward Gerald, as if to ask advice, when she saw him gravely going through the same ceremony. She did not speak until they were again riding side by side, when she said in a strained surprised tone:

"Surely, Mr. Keithly, you do not believe in any such ceremony as the one I have just witnessed."

He laughed heartily at her tone. "Surely, Miss Genevieve," he replied, "when I am in Rome I strive to do as Rome does when the doing so does not harm me nor any one else. The Indians believe that the water will keep off the disease, and they have an inkling of the truth. I don't mean to say that I believe the sprinkling of water, as I did just now, will have any effect, either good or bad, on the human system; but it is declared in Holy Writ that 'Cleanliness is next to godliness,' and truly a clean body is almost proof against disease."

"But don't you think that by participating in their strange ceremonies, you only encourage the Indians to keep up their barbaric customs?" Genevieve asked.

"What was wrong with this ceremony?" he asked by way of reply. "Surely you would not wish to deprive these people of all their customs and ceremonies. The ceremony to-day was simple and innocent; there was no harm done to any one—and if it pleases them to keep such a custom, I say, let them do so. Now, if it were the scalp-dance or war-dance or any of their ceremonies calculated to harm themselves or others, I should use all my influence in blotting it out; but these Indians have long ago laid aside their savage, cruel customs and have no more desire to practice them than we have to see them do so."

"Right, as ever," said Genevieve, frankly extending her hand. "I did not think of it as you present the matter; but I see I should have strengthened my influence over my Indian friends, by pleasing them in performing their water-ceremony. It seems I can never see things as they are, in the true light."

"Now don't blame yourself so. I'll act 'father confessor,' and give absolution if you wish; you took the same view of the case that many others of our race have taken, and you have not done any harm. I may be wrong in the view I take of the matter," he added, "but I have thought often and long over it, and my course seems best to me."

"And to me," she hastened to say. "I think if we always do what seems best to us, after investigating to the best of our ability, and praying it all out to the great 'Father confessor,' we shall not go far wrong." There was a mist in her eyes as she said this in a low tone.

"Amen," he exclaimed soberly and reverently.

This gave the conversation a more serious turn and the speakers a kindlier regard for each other.

8

What Became of It?

"Gerald Keithly, where is the money these poor Indians should have had on their head-right long ago?" asked sturdy Choe Harjo of his guest one evening, as Keithly was spending the night with him.

"The per-capita payment that should have been made and was not?" Gerald asked.

"Yes," Choe answered. "My people here are in destitute circumstances, some of them wanting the necessaries of life, and have been anxiously looking forward to this payment. John Darrel, the merchant of Samilla, came through here last week and told me that the delegates whom we sent to represent us at Washington had acted treacherously and that we would get no money. He gave Mihia some papers, and she tried to explain it all to me but I cannot understand it exactly."

"Miss Genevieve, do you understand what he says?" asked Keithly turning to Genevieve who sat quietly crocheting.

She looked up smiling. "Yes; you were talking about the per-capita payment. Would you like to see the papers?" and she rose to get them.

"No, it is not necessary. I have read several accounts of the 'robbery' as it is called."

Then turning to Choe who was waiting his reply, he said: "I do not know that I can explain the matter satisfactorily, for the accounts of the newspapers are not clear. The fact that is most evident to all, is that the money has been unlawfully used, by the delegates and the Indians will never derive any benefit from it. How, when, or where the delegates obtained possession of this money has not yet been explained; but the newspapers published here denounce the actions of these men intrusted with the affairs of the government, in strong language, calling the affair a 'robbery' and the actors, 'thieves.' Still, they do not prove anything, and so the matter rests."

"My people collected in the grove and asked me about this matter," Choe Harjo said after a silence. "I told them what Mihia and John Darrel had told me, and they were very angry and disappointed. They say if these men do not explain their conduct, they will investigate the matter and 'make it hot' for them when they get back. I fear trouble and bloodshed will yet result from this."

"Yes, I am afraid so. The people in and around my school are holding secret meetings and passing resolutions that, if carried out, will seriously incommode these criminal officials. I attended one of their meetings the other evening and felt rather uncomfortable over the warmth and feeling they expressed. You would have liked one of the speeches," turning to Genevieve, "for it was a real 'oration against Cataline.' Cicero himself could not have waxed more eloquent in denouncing the enemy in the Roman camp, the traitor Cataline, than did this ignorant savage, in accusing his treacherous officials. The speaker was an old, gray-haired Indian, feeble and tottering, but his voice was clear and resonant and his face beamed with emotion. Said he: 'Years ago, so many that I cannot count them, before we left the dear home in Alabama, when I was young, a delegate was sent from our tribe to represent us, and to watch our interests in the great capital. The United States wanted to buy our lands and send us up to this little spot where we now are, but we would not sell, for we knew nothing of the land in the west, and we loved our home. Our delegate was one of our wisest, and we thought, best men, and we instructed him not to listen to any proposition the United States should make; for if he did, and did sell our land, we said, we would kill him when he returned. He promised that he would do as we instructed him and listen to no terms the United States should make in regard to buying our land; but after he came back we found that he had acted treacherously and that we were homeless. Oh, the bitterness of that hour! The Indians with one accord gathered around the beautiful residence of the traitor and calling for him to come forth, took him and bound him. Upon his asking what their conduct meant, they answered: "Thus punisheth the Indians all traitors. You have made us homeless; we will make you lifeless; you sold our lands and filled your pockets with the defiled gold; we will make you poorer than when an infant you lay upon your mother's breast. Thus perish all traitors!" and we shot him through and through until there was no flesh to mark a bullet. Then making a bonfire of his home, we separated, satisfied. Soon we moved to this country. I am an old man and see things in a different light from what you younger men do; but it seems to me the Indian's honor should be as sacred to-night as it was on the night we slew our delegate for treachery and dishonesty. If I understand this matter correctly, our delegates and chief received our head-right money and can make no satisfactory explanation concerning the use they make of it. It belonged to the people; let the people have it, if not by gentle means, then let us use forcible means.'

"This speech aroused the hearers to such a frenzy of emotion that had the chief and delegates been present, I fear there would have been four Indians less; at any rate, they resolved to wait upon these offending parties, and demand an explanation, and if that were not satisfactory, serve them with the same sauce of powder and shot with which their former delegate was served. I hear the meetings have become universal, and a caucus is held in every locality; and if the chief and delegates do not remain away there will not be enough left of them to 'mark the spot whereon they lie.' "

So spoke and thought this friend of the red man.

The wrath of the Indians waxed hotter and hotter, and their secret meetings became more numerous, when at this time the delegates returned. When called upon for an explanation of their actions, they answered that they would explain all, at the session of council which the chief would call together soon. At this session, no one was present but the chief, the delegates, and the members of the Houses who were all implicated, for those who went determined to thoroughly investigate the matter came away, "mum" and apparently satisfied. Who can declare with truth that money is not a power which the rulers of the world cannot withstand?

The confused and contradictory statements of the criminal delegates were received in silence, and so the matter rested. Not an arm was raised in defence of the poor Indians stripped of their bread-money, notwithstanding the mutterings of dissatisfaction and threats of vengeance heard all along the lines; and thus a great robbery passed into oblivion.

But the Indians learned a lesson therefrom, and they were not the only learners.

9

Some Changes

"Wynema, I am going home this vacation, and want you to go with me; would you like to go?" asked Miss Weir one morning, as she and Wynema were on their way to the school-house.

By the way, this school-house deserves some notice, for a great change has taken place in it. In place of the little log-cabin, chinked with mud, stood a large frame building, constructed from the most approved modern plan and furnished with every convenience. The attendance had grown so large that another teacher had to be employed, and Wynema, who was at that time well qualified to fill the position, was chosen in preference to a stranger. And the change did not stop with the school-house, for everywhere, all around their building, were neat residences in place of the tepees; and to the right of the school-building stood a fine new church, adorned with steeple and bell, whose sound called together the people every sabbath to worship beneath the arched roof of the holy edifice. Miss Weir had organized a sabbath-school which met in the school-house, soon after she came among these people; but the school increased so much in numbers that she hardly recognized in it her small beginning. White people had settled among these Indians, and being peaceful and law-abiding, the Indians welcomed them and gave them a helping hand. A young missionary, Carl Peterson by name, a

34

teacher in Mr. Keithly's school, came over every Sabbath and expounded Scripture to an attentive congregation. This same missionary deserves mention, as he had toiled five years among the Sioux Indians, and was giving his whole life to spreading the Gospel among the Indians.

This little village of Tepees had grown so much that its inhabitants wished to dignify it by a name whose orthography English-speaking people could master, and by a post-office. So they applied to Miss Weir to know if she would object to having the town called for her.

"No," said she; "Weir does not sound well as the name of a town; but if you do not care, I will suggest another and a better. Call it Wynema. That is pretty enough for any town," and so it was called.

But we have wandered afar off and must return to the present.

Wynema looked wistfully at the one whom she still called Mihia, and clasping her hands said:

"Oh, wouldn't I? Oh, Mihia. To go with you among your people, to see your dear mother, your brother, and sisters of whom you often tell me—that would be joy; but my poor father and mother! what would become of them if I should never return?"

"But we shall come back, Wynema. I am coming back if God spares me. Your mother and father will be glad to have you see something of the world beyond this little village, and I know they would rather trust you with me than with any one. Only consent to go and all can be arranged for us to have a pleasant trip and visit. My little girl has grown so dear to me that I dislike to part with her for even a short while,"—and Genevieve placed her hand on her friend's arm.

That stroke won the battle and Genevieve had her way. The friends talked animatedly of their projected visit until they reached home that afternoon, after the school duties were performed. The plan was submitted to Wynema's parents' inspection, and after some natural reluctance they gave it their hearty approval. Then as the holidays were near, preparations were made for the friends' departure.

10

Gerald Speaks

"Are you sick, Monsieur Gerald, that you are so pale and quiet? You have not asked me a question when you generally ask me so many," teased Wynema. The years had turned the tables and made her the tease. "Did you know that Miss Genevieve and I are going back to her home on a visit, in a few weeks? Yes? Who told you? We can never surprise you, for I believe you keep a particular courier running back and forth all the time to keep you informed concerning our doings and misdoings."

He smiled at her quietly. "It seems our little girl—by the way, that is now a *misnomer*—is glad to go away and leave us; are you, Wynema? But, of course, you will deny it. I am not glad to see you go, for I shall miss you sadly. Do you know why I came here to-day? Now, see if you are not so good a guesser as I am."

"Why, to see us to be sure—*Mihia* I mean," she said in a lower tone. "It does not take great perceptive faculties to know that."

"Yes, to see you; but more than that, I came to take you back with *me* to spend the day. To-morrow will be Saturday, and you can offer no excuse which I will accept."

"Oh, as to that matter, we—or that is I—shall be delighted to go if Miss Genevieve will go also. What do you say Mihia?"

she asked turning to Genevieve who was listening with a smile at her raillery.

"That nothing could please me better at present than a visit to Keithly College, and that I thank your Monsieur Gerald for giving us this pleasure," she answered smilingly.

"It is I who am thankful, for I receive the benefit and pleasure," Gerald said looking gravely toward Genevieve.

The road leading to Keithly College was very short, it seemed to the three friends, bowling merrily along. Soon the college loomed up in sight, a beautiful and stately edifice. The girls stopped in the grounds to admire. "Oh, how beautiful! How lovely! How perfectly magnificent," cried Wynema, clapping her hands together in admiration of every beautiful object about her. "See that beautiful fountain, Mihia," pointing to one formed of three ducks with their heads thrown upward, together making the spray. This fountain stood in the center of a small, artificial lake, on an island formed of rocks and shells.

"Now, Miss Superlative Adjective, are you not ready to go in?" Gerald asked Wynema after they had walked over the grounds. "I assure you the teachers are anxious to see Miss Weir, and perhaps *one* of them desires to see Miss Wynema," he added teasingly.

They entered the house and met the teachers and pupils who were expecting them.

"You see, Carl, I brought them," Keithly said to Peterson. "Miss Wynema," he added, turning to her with mock gravity "this is the courier whom I keep running to and fro to inform me of your doings. He told me about your going and seemed very doleful about it; ask him."

Carl turned to Wynema whom he greatly admired, and began talking about other topics to hide his confusion. The teachers and pupils scattered over the house and grounds enjoying the beautiful weather.

Gerald Keithly drew Genevieve Weir away, saying:

"I have a beautiful plant in full bloom which I wish to show you, Miss Weir, and as it stands on the balcony beyond the alcove, I suppose 'Mohamet will have to go to the mountain;' see?—here it is; how do you like it?"

It was a beautiful plant of a variety Genevieve had never seen, for Mr. Keithly was a botanist and greatly loved flowers and sought out all strange, new varieties.

The foliage was variegated, dark and light green, and the flowers which grew in large clusters were deep scarlet in the centers and shading out to pale pink petals. Genevieve feasted her eyes on its beauties before she answered:

"Magnificent beyond compare," she said at last with a half-sigh. "What do you call it? La Reine? That is what it should be called, for it is the queen of flowers, surely."

"Just as you are the queen among women," thought Gerald, but he said: "So you like it? I thought you would. I was going to carry it to you when I heard you were going home, so I brought you to see it."

She had seated herself in the window on the balcony, and he sat down beside her. They were silent for some time, when Gerald said in an altered tone:

"Would you like to live here, Genevieve? You have often said you liked the place. Could you content yourself to spend your life here, dear?"

Genevieve looked at him wonderingly. "I do not know what you mean, Mr. Keithly," she said.

"What I mean? I mean that I love you with all my heart and strength; that next to my Creator, you are the dearest being in the universe to me; that I love you better than my own life, for it would be unbearable without your dear presence; and I mean that I want you forever and ever for my own, dear, little wife,"—ah, how tenderly he spoke! "That is what I have meant since I first saw you, but I could not tell you until I found that you were to be taken from me, and I feared I should never see you again. Oh, my darling, the very thought of separation sickens me. I feel that I cannot bear it at all unless you promise me you will come back as mine, my little girl, my darling wife. Do you love me at all, dear?" and Gerald kissed the hand he held in his own.

Genevieve seemed struggling for utterance. How could she hurt the dear, noble man who now stood before her with his deep, honest love beaming from every feature; but she must make him understand somehow that his request could never, no, *never* be granted, she said to herself; finally she said:

"No, my dear, dear friend. It can never be; I am sorry—*so* sorry for your sake that things have turned out as they have!"

"Why, Genevieve, do you love another?" he interposed.

"Yes," she said and blushed.

"Tell me about it," Gerald demanded resignedly.

"There is not much to tell," Genevieve complied—"only that Maurice Mauran and I have been sweethearts almost from childhood. We are not engaged, for I would not have it so though he urged long and earnestly. I thought it best to test our love by separation, for if it stands the test of time it is true. We have neither of us married, and Maurice is still waiting for me," she ended with a deeper flush.

"And if your love stands the test, you will be married?" he questioned.

"Yes; and we will accompany Wynema home. If not, I shall come back anyhow."

He made no reply as she turned to join the others. "Wait," he said laying a detaining hand on her arm; "I may write to you, sometimes?"

"Yes," she responded, looking frankly in his eyes, "as friend to friend."

"I hope I shall not forget—" he began proudly,—then seeing her pained expression he cried, "forgive me, Genevieve, I am hardly responsible for what I say."

Then they joined the others and hid their emotions in forced gayety.

II

In the Old Home

"Oh, how nice it is to be home again!" cried Genevieve, looking into every remembered nook and cranny about the place. "Nothing changed, but everything seems to nod a familiar 'How d'ye do.' I declare, I don't feel a day older than when I ran up the attic stairs and crawled out of the window into the old elm tree, where Robin and I had our 'Robinson Crusoe's house,' and I was the 'man Friday.' Do you remember the day you fell out, Robin, when the bear got after you and you climbed out on the bough, when it broke? It would seem as yesterday if Robin were not such a tall, broad-shouldered fellow, really towering over us all; and I, a cross-grained, wrinkled spinster; and Toots putting on young lady's airs — I suppose we shall have to call her Bessie, now; and even Winnie, our dear, little baby, is laying aside her dolls and — I do really believe it, Miss — is smiling at Charley or Willie or Ted. Ah, no wonder the little Mith feels so ancient when she views such a group of grown folks and realizes they are her children. But let's hear a report of yourselves, and I'll satisfy the baby's curiosity to see my Indian relics," — and a laughing, happy group, they recount experiences, compare notes and enjoy themselves generally.

Back at the old home, Genevieve is the light-hearted girl of long ago, to be teased and petted, and to tease and pet in return. And in all this merriment and happiness is our little Indian friend forgotten or pushed aside because of her dark skin and savage manners? Ah, no; she is the friend of their dear one, and for that reason, at first, she was warmly welcomed and graciously entertained, and afterward she was loved for her own good qualities. Many were the rambles and rides, the drives and picnics these young people enjoyed. Generally Robin, Bessie and Wynema formed these excursion parties, for Genevieve preferred remaining at home or had a "previous engagement."

After "the visitor," —as Winnie still called Wynema much to her discomfiture and amusement—had been with them for some weeks, she and Robin, with Winnie for propriety, for Bessie was detained at home, were out rowing on the bay, when Robin glancing up at his companion, asked: "Doesn't the rippling of the waves make your head swim? make you 'drunk' as Winnie says?"

"No, I am accustomed to being on the water; I often row alone. I don't ever remember of feeling 'drunk.' What kind of a feeling is it?" she smiled inquiringly.

"Oh, I can't tell exactly—only you feel as if the ground were slipping from under you, and the world and everything therein, spinning like a top for your amusement. It isn't a pleasant feeling, I assure you," and he put his hand to his head as if he were then experiencing the feeling.

"No, I presume not, from your description. But where and how did you gain so much information about it? Personal experience?" mischievously.

"No," Winnie spoke up in defense of her favorite, "Robin never was drunk. But Mr. Snifer, oh, he gets just awful drunk, and he just falls down, and fights his wife, and I'm awful afraid of him," clasping her hands earnestly.

"Thank you, Pet, for defending my character," said her brother lovingly. "You see, Miss Wynema, our little girl has been studying grammar and makes much progress."

"I am sure of one thing," said Wynema, taking the child's hand; "that is, though this little maid may not be perfectly correct in the use of words, she will never be deficient in the depth of her affection. Dear, I am sorry your neighbor is such a beastly man; but that reminds me of some of my people when they become intoxicated—'get drunk,' as you term it—only my people act much worse. They ride through the streets, firing pistols and whooping loudly, and often kill many people. 'Firewater' is an awful thing among your people who are more civilized than we are, and you can imagine what a terrible influence it exerts among my people." The child shuddered and shut her eyes.

"But, Miss Wynema—"

"Don't call me that; I am not accustomed to it," she interrupted.

"Well, but Wynema, I thought it was against the law of the United States to carry whisky or any intoxicant into your country," Robin said surprisedly.

"So it is against the treaty made by the U. S. government with the Indians; but, notwithstanding all this, the whisky is brought into our country and sold to our people."

"Are not the smugglers ever apprehended and punished?" he asked.

"Oh, yes, often; but that does not materially affect the unholy and unlawful practice. Only last Christmas, as your sister can tell you better than I, drunken Indians and white men were to be seen on the streets of all our towns. Oh, it is terrible," shuddering. "The only way I can see, of exterminating the evil is to pull it up by the roots; stop the manufacture and of necessity the sale of it will be stopped."

"I believe you would make a staunch Woman's Christian Temperance Unionist, for that is their argument," he replied admiringly.

"Indeed, I am a member of that union. We have a small union in our town and do all we can against the great evil— intemperance; but what can a little band of women, prohibited from voting against the ruin of their husbands, sons and firesides, do, when even the great government of Uncle Sam is set at defiance?" Wynema waxed eloquent in defense of her "hobby."

"I am afraid you are a regular suffragist!" Robin said, shrugging his shoulders.

"So I am," emphatically; "but it does me very little good, only for the principle's sake. Still, I believe that, one day, the 'inferior of man,' the 'weaker vessel' shall stand grandly by the side of that 'noble lord of creation,' his equal in *every* respect."

"Hear! Hear! How much the 'cause' loses by not having you to publicly advocate it! Say, didn't sister teach you all this along with the rest? I think you must have imbibed those strong suffrage principles and ideas from her," said Robin, teasingly.

She went on earnestly, ignoring his jesting manner: "Your sister and I hold many opinions in common, and doubtless, I have imbibed some of hers, as I have the greatest respect for her opinions; but the idea of freedom and liberty was born in me. It is true the women of my country have no voice in the councils; we do not speak in any public gathering, not even in our churches; but we are waiting for our more civilized white sisters to gain their liberty, and thus set us an example which we shall not be slow to follow." She finished, her cheeks flushed and her eyes sparkling with earnestness and animation. Robin looked at her with admiration shining in his dark blue eyes.

"I am sure of that, if you are a fair representative of your people," he said. "But I will not jest about the matter any longer, for I am as truly interested in it as you are. I think it will only be a matter of time, and a short time, too, when the question as to whether our women may participate in our liberties, help choose our officers, even our presidents, will be settled in their favor—at least, I hope so. There is no man who is enterprising and keeps well up with the times but confesses that the women of to-day are in every respect, except political liberty, equal to the men. It could not be successfully denied, for college statistics prove it by showing the number of women who have borne off the honors, even when public sentiment was against them and in favor of their brother-competitors. And not alone in an intellectual sense are you women our equals, but you have the energy and ambition, and far more morality than we can claim. Then you know so well how to put your learning in practice. See the college graduates who make successful farmers, vintners, etc. Indeed, you women can do anything you wish," he said, in a burst of admiration.

"Except to vote," she replied quietly.

"And you would do that if I had my way," Robin said warmly.

"It seems to me somebody else would make a splendid lecturer on Woman's Rights. You had better enlist," tauntingly.

"By taking one of the women? I should like to," and he looked into her eyes his deep meaning.

12

A Conservative

Soon after Genevieve's return, Maurice Mauran came over to bid her welcome, and to renew the tie that once bound them, but which Genevieve severed when she departed to dwell among the Indians. Genevieve was rejoiced to be with him again, and noted all changes in him for the better, with pride and delight; but she noticed his indifferent and slighting manner of speaking about religion and secular matters, temperance and her much-loved Indians; and it troubled her. All the questions of the day were warmly discussed during his visits, which were of frequent occurrence, when finally, a short while before Genevieve's departure, the subject of woman's suffrage came up, and Genevieve warmly defended it.

"Why, Genevieve," said Maurice, "I fear you are a 'real live,' suffragist! I wonder that you have not cut off your hair and started out on a lecturing tour; I'm sure you would do well. Really, little girl," he said more seriously, "you are too pronounced in your opinions on all subjects. Don't you know ladies are not expected to have any ideas except about housekeeping, fancy-work, dress and society, until after they are married, when they only echo the opinions of their husbands? As for woman's rights, I don't want my little wife to bother her head about that, for it is immodest and unwomanly. You look surprised, but what would a woman out of her sphere be, but unwomanly?"

"I look and am surprised, Maurice, at your statement," Genevieve replied quietly. "I am surprised that a man of your culture could entertain such 'old-fogy' opinions as you have expressed. It is just such and like sentiments that have held women back into obscurity for so long; but, thank God!" she added fervently, "sensible men are beginning to open their eyes and see things in a different light from what their ancestors saw them. The idea of a woman being unwomanly and immodest because she happens to be thoughtful and to have 'two ideas above an oyster,' to know a little beyond and above house and dress is perfectly absurd and untrue. Is Mrs. Hayes, wife of ex-president Hayes, and president of the Woman's Mission Board immodest because she does not devote her time to cleaning house or planning dresses, but prefers doing missionary work? And is the great leader of temperance work, Frances E. Willard, World's and National president of the Woman's Christian Temperance Union, of whom one of your great men said 'I think she is one of the most remarkable women the century has produced,' and another called her 'that peerless woman of the earth, that uncrowned queen,'—I say, is she unwomanly because she prefers to devote her life to temperance work instead of keeping house for some man for her 'victuals and clothes?' As for that matter, who of our leaders, our truly great women, can be truthfully called immodest or unwomanly? Their very womanliness is their passport to the hearts of their fellow-men—their insurance of success. Ah, my friend, you will have to change your opinion on this question for a newer and better one, for yours is decidedly old-fashioned and out of taste," she concluded warmly.

"Well, we won't quarrel about it, for I know you are not so interested in these questions as to be disagreeable about them.

I don't and cannot believe in a woman coming out in public in any capacity; but so long as I have my little wife at home, I will keep my sentiments to myself."

And the subject passed without more notice; but the seeds of discord were planted in the hearts of the two who were "Two children in a hamlet bred and born," and should have been "Two hearts that beat as one."

It seemed very strange to Genevieve that she should be constantly comparing Maurice Mauran to Gerald Keithly, and not always in Maurice's favor. She thought how differently these two men believed, and one was buried among the Indians where it would be thought he had no opportunity for keeping up with the times; and still—and then she sighed and did not finish.

13

Shall We Allot?

"What is it you are reading, Mihia, that you look so troubled?" queried Wynema coming in one afternoon from a stroll she had taken with Robert and Bessie, and looking very pretty with her bright, merry eyes and rosy cheeks. She came and looked over her friend's shoulder in her loving way. "Oh, what a long article!" drawing down her face. "Shall we allot? allot what? Oh, that is a home paper! Surely it cannot mean allot our country?"

"That is just what it means, dear," replied her friend. "Some United States Senators are very much in favor of allotting in severalty the whole of the Indian Territory, and, of course, that would take in your country also. I don't like the idea, though it has been talked of for a long time. It seems to me a plan by which the 'boomers' who were left out of Oklahoma are to be landed. For years the U. S. Senators and citizens have been trying to devise ways and means by which to divide the Indians' country, but, as yet, nothing has been done. Now the matter assumes a serious aspect, for even the part-blood Indians are in favor of allotment; and if the Indians do not stand firmly against it, I fear they will yet be homeless," and Miss Weir sighed and gazed abstractedly at her listener.

"But I don't see how dividing our lands can materially damage us," said Wynema looking thoughtfully back again.

"We should have our own homes, and contrary to ruining our fortunes I think it would mend them. See! This is the way I see the matter. If I am wrong, correct me. There are so many idle, shiftless Indians who do nothing but hunt and fish; then there are others who are industrious and enterprising; so long as our land remains as a whole, in common, these lazy Indians will never make a move toward cultivating it; and the industrious Indians and 'squaw men' will inclose as much as they can for their own use. Thus the land will be unequally divided, the lazy Indians getting nothing because they will not exert themselves to do so; while, if the land were allotted, do you not think that these idle Indians, knowing the land to be their own, would have pride enough to cultivate their land and build up their homes? It seems so to me;" and she looked earnestly at Genevieve, awaiting her reply.

"I had not thought of the matter in the way you present it, though that is the view many congressmen and editors take of it. Then again in support of your theory that allotment will be best, this paper says the Indians *must* allot, to protect themselves against the U. S. Government, and suggests that the more civilized apply for statehood; for it says 'if the protection provided for in the treaties be insufficient, more certain protection should be secured.' Another paper says, 'Gen. Noble, Secretary of the Interior, in his recent report, strikes a blow at "Wild West" shows by recommending an act of congress, forbidding any person or corporation to take into employment or under control any American Indian. He advocates a continuance of the policy of exclusion in connection with the Indian Territory cattle question; suggests that the period now allowed a tribe to determine whether it will receive allotment be placed under the control of the President, so that it may be shortened if *tribes give no attention to the subject or cause unreasonable delays*; and discountenances the employment of attorneys by the Indians to aid in negotiations with, or to prosecute claims against, the government.' This sounds like the lands will be allotted whether the Indians like or no. I cannot see the matter as it has been presented by you, and as these papers advocate it, my idea is, that it will be the ruin of the poor, ignorant savage. It will do very well for the civilized tribes, but they should never consent to it until their weaker brothers are willing and able. Laws are made for people and not people for laws. The South Sea Islander could not be governed by the laws of England, nor can the North American Indian become a fit subject of the United States. Do you not see, my friend, that if your land were divided, your territory would then become a state—a subject of the United States Government. Do you think the western tribes sufficiently tutored in the school of civilization to become citizens of the United States, subject to its laws and punishments?"

"Oh, no indeed! Far from it! What a superficial thinker I am not to have understood this!" answered the girl vehemently.

"Then there is another objection to this measure," continued Miss Weir, "that seems very weighty to me. Were the land divided, these poor, ignorant, improvident, short-sighted Indians would be persuaded and threatened into selling their homes, piece by piece, perhaps, until finally they would be homeless outcasts, and then what would become of 'Poor Lo!' None of his white brothers, who so sweetly persuaded away his home, would give him a night's shelter or a morsel of food." Genevieve was so intensely earnest that she had risen and was pacing the room, her hands clasped together, her brows knit. Wynema, who seldom saw her in such moods, was frightened, and reproached herself with having been the cause of it.

"Oh, I am so sorry, dear Mihia—so sorry I was so foolish! Pray, forgive me! It is always the way with me, and I dare say I should be one of the first to sell myself out of house and home;" and the girl hung her head, looking the picture of humiliation.

"No, dear, I am the one to ask forgiveness for needlessly disturbing you so. Now go along and enjoy yourself, for I dare say nothing will come of all this;" and Genevieve kissed her friend, hoping that she might never have cause to be less light-hearted than at present.

14

More Concerning Allotments

When Maurice Mauran came over to make his accustomed visit, Genevieve brought up the subject of allotment, incidentally, and showed him the paper she had been reading. She spoke calmly and indifferently, striving to hide her own sentiments that she might obtain his free opinion.

"You are an able lawyer, one of the lights of your profession, and more able to form a correct opinion as to whether it would be legal for the United States Government to allot the Indians' land against the expressed desire of this people."

When he had finished reading, he threw the paper down, saying, "Pshaw! I hope you do not waste your time reading such stuff as this. Why, don't you see that this allotment would be the best thing that ever happened to the Indian, for it would bring him out and educate him? As it is, he will remain just as he is and has been since the 'year one,' — nothing but an uncouth savage. Why, don't you know, Genevieve, the Indian in an uncivilized state is nothing more than a brute? He hasn't as much sense as Prince, there," pointing to his dog which came and laid his head on his master's knee. "You see he understands that I am talking about him; don't you, old fellow. And if," said he, resuming his argument, "if by constant contact and intercourse with white people the Indians do not become civilized, why, let them go to the dogs, I say, for they are not worth spending time and money on; and what is the use of their cumbering lands that white people might be cultivating? Why, what's the matter with you, Genevieve? you look as if you had been struck," he said suddenly turning to her.

"Nothing is the matter," she replied in an ominously quiet tone. "I am waiting for you to go on. I want to hear your full opinion."

"Well, then don't look at me so;" she withdrew her eyes. "I am afraid, Genevieve," he went on, "that your sojourn among the Indians was not at all beneficial to you. You will excuse me, I hope, for saying it, but I don't want my affianced wife to hold such opinions regarding so important a matter as this Indian question, as you evidently hold. You lived among them; you know them to be idle, trifling, a people whom no amount of cultivation could civilize, and yet you wish to go back and add to the disgrace of your former stay among them. Forgive me, my dear girl, if I offend you by my plain language, but it is best we should understand each other. I cannot but feel it a disgrace for you to have lived and labored among such a people—a people very little superior to the negro in my opinion. I am fond of you, you know, and proud of your gifted mind, but I do not want my wife to stock her mind with sentiments that, if held by all, would be injurious to the commonwealth." He spoke in the patronizing way men usually adopt when reasoning with women. "I have looked forward to your home-coming and comforted myself during our separation with the thought that soon that separation would be over forever; that, one in mind and heart we would wander peacefully down the hill of time together, and side by side rest at its foot when our journey is done; but despite my great affection for you, my dear, I cannot overlook—"

"Stop!" cried Genevieve, her eyes flashing and her cheeks flaming with indignation. "I have had enough of that. I asked you your opinion on the Indian question and instead you are giving me the model by which you expect to mold your future wife. You had better get one of clay or putty as that will turn into any shape you wish to mold it. You say I have disgraced myself by laboring among the ignorant, idle, treacherous Indians; but never in all the years I have dwelt among these savages have I been subjected to the insult your words imply. I asked you for an opinion; you have given me vituperation; and not being content with slandering the poor, ignorant, defenseless Indians, you begin on me. Oh, if I pretended to be a man, I'd be a *man*, and not a sniveling coward. If you were a man, I would reason with you, but you do not understand the first principles of logic. Your wife, indeed! I have never promised to be such, and please heaven! I never will. My husband must be a man, full-grown—a man capable of giving an opinion, just and honest, without using insult to do so. Good evening! I have no time to spend in arguing about a people who have not the intellect of a dog," and with a curl of her lip, and a toss of the head, she swept from the room, righteously angry.

The young man, left to himself, was hardly able to conduct himself to the door, for so sudden had been Genevieve's attack that it left him stunned with surprise—not so stunned, however, but that he was able to understand that his long-cherished hope of "owning" this girl was crushed forever.

There was no mistaking the tone of her voice and her emphatic words.

Very different from his opinion was that of Gerald Keithly as expressed in a letter which she received a few days after her quarrel with Maurice. He said:

"You will see by this that I am still with my charge. I did not get off as I desired, for the country is so disturbed over the threatened measure—allotment in severalty—that I thought it best to stay and see the matter settled, though I do not believe the land will be divided soon. I think it is a mere question of time, when it will be; and God knows what will become of these poor savages when it is! For, as you know, they have so little providence or shrewdness or any kind of business sense, that their sharper white brothers would soon show them 'the way the land lies.' I cannot but admit that this measure would be best for the half-bloods and those educated in the ways of the world, able to fight their own battles; but it would be the ruin of the poor, ignorant full-bloods. 'The strong should protect the weak' says chivalry; but there seems to be very little if any chivalric spirit shown in the case of these Indians. Little Fox came over yesterday to ask my opinion concerning the probability of the passage of this measure. I told him just what I thought about it, and he said, straightening back proudly: 'But the United States Government cannot take our lands and divide them, for they are ours. They made a treaty with us to the effect that this land should be ours and our children's so long as grass grows and water runs; if it be ours, what right has congress to take it and divide it? They cannot force us to divide, against our will, legally, either, and we will never consent to this measure. We know what it means. It means statehood first, and it means homeless Indians, last. Have not the white people pushed us farther and farther away, until now we are in this little corner of the world? And do they now wish to deprive us of it? Why do they not go to Texas when homes are offered for the making, and a welcome extended to the homeless? Do you think the whites would furnish us homes if we gave them ours? Not much. No, we will never agree to this measure; I will fight it with my last breath,' he added fiercely.

" 'Well,' I said, 'if you all stand firmly against this measure it cannot be passed legally, for that would stake the honor of the United States Government. But the Indians can be threatened and bribed into agreeing to divide their lands; and the tide is so

15

Wynema's Mischief

"Mother," said Genevieve Weir one day, "I feel that I must leave you. I have staid longer than I at first intended, for it was so sweet and pleasant to be with you all again; but now my people, 'even my people, Israel'," she quoted seriously, "need me and I must go. Perhaps I shall not stay so long as before. I cannot tell, for now we are civilized and you can make the next visit. I do wish you would come, mother dear, for I assure you would meet with the warmest welcome from my Indian friends."

"But, dear," replied her mother, "I thought you were come to stay. Is there anything wrong between you and Maurice?"

"Nothing wrong, mother dear, all is right; at last I have learned before it was too late that he was not fitted to become my husband. We are so entirely dissimilar that we could never be happy together, and so we have 'agreed to disagree'—the only thing we ever agreed upon," and she turned her face aside that her mother might not read there a deeper meaning.

"Genevieve, I am very sorry for this, for I had hoped so earnestly to keep my little girl with me; and I knew if you married Maurice he would keep you; but if you do not love him you would not be happy, and I should be the last to advise you to marry him. But, oh! I miss you so and am so uneasy about you, so far away from home. Suppose you should get sick? Are you sure, Genevieve, that your friend Mr. Keithly, whom you esteem so highly, does not in any way come between you and Maurice?"

Genevieve had been standing with bowed head, but now she looked down earnestly and frankly into her mother's eyes.

"Oh, no, indeed!" she exclaimed vehemently. "What makes you think so, mother? Gerald Keithly is only a friend, a very good friend of mine. I have often told you of his kindness to me, as you know, but I have never thought of loving him."

Mrs. Weir looked into her daughter's eyes and doubted her not, though she wondered what caused the estrangement between her and Maurice who now came only occasionally, and when Genevieve was away.

"My dear, I yearn to keep you, but I know it is only throwing words away to urge you, when you feel it your duty to go. So I place you in the dear Lord's keeping, knowing that He can care for you far better than I." Genevieve stooped and kissed her mother.

"That is the best way, dearest, to think of it. But you have not asked me when I am going. I shall start the day after to-morrow if all things are favorable."

In the meantime we are forgetting Wynema, and leaving her out in the cold. But if we are neglectful of her, there is some one who is not. Robin Weir, Genevieve's only brother, tall, fair and handsome, broad-shouldered and twenty-five, the pride and joy of his sisters, had fallen desperately in love with "the little Indian," as he termed her before he knew her; but the moment his blue eyes rested on the witching, mischievous dark-eyed little beauty, he became her willing subject, and followed her about everywhere, greatly to her delight and amusement—for Indians are sometimes coquettish.

The day before her departure, Robin found her high up in

the old cherry-tree poring over a volume of Tennyson's poems, totally absorbed and oblivious of her surroundings.

"Phew! I wonder how you got up there!" he called to her. She looked up but did not seem startled.

"Why?" she questioned. "Do you wish to come up too? Well, sir, I put my foot on the lowest bough and leapt up. I am sure there is no art about that;" and she laughed merrily.

"No," said he dubiously, "but there must be a great deal of agility. Say; I'd like to see you do it again."

"Now, there is scheming for you! No, sir, I am not going to please you so much, though I am not afraid but that I could get up as readily as at first. Did you never read that Pocahontas could leap from one tree to another like a squirrel?"

"Yes, but you are not Pocahontas, and I am not John Smith, though I wish I were."

"Why?" she asked, amusedly curious.

"For then you would jump down and save me—from toiling up this tree. But if I must, I must. So, here goes!" and he placed his hand on the bough and vaulted up lightly.

"Well done!" she cried, clasping her hands. "I knew you could if you only tried, and—"

"And so you would not help me any," he interrupted. "You would not have cared if I had hurt myself," he said in a lower tone. "What is that you are reading?"

"Oh, just one of Tennyson's poems!" she replied closing the book and keeping her finger in it.

"But which one?" he persisted, reaching for the book. "Let me see it. I'd like to see your favorites, and I know it must have been one, for you were so absorbed in it;" and he took the book from her, closing it as he did so. He turned the pages trying to find the poem he supposed she had been reading, and not being able to do so, looked up. There was a smile of triumph in Wynema's dark eyes as they met his, but she lowered them when she saw the passion in his, and a crimson tide colored her cheeks and brow. He grasped her hand warmly saying:

"Wynema, little girl, won't you tell me which it was? I know. It was Elaine, for here are—why do you cry, darling? Did you think of our parting to-morrow? Sweetheart, my farewell speech to you is that of Elaine to Launcelot—'Not to be with you, not to see your face—alas, for me, then, my good days are done!' Tell me, darling, will you think of me when you are back among your friends? You never would tell me whether you love me, though you know I love you devotedly. Tell me now, won't you?" he pleaded.

"Why, Robin, there are visitors at the house!" she exclaimed looking interestedly toward the house.

"Well, let them be; I don't want to see them," he answered impatiently.

"Oh, how cross we are! I shall have to leave Robin until he gets into a better humor;" and she made a movement to go; but he threw his arm across and prevented her.

"No; you shall not go till you answer my question; you have evaded it long enough, and I must have an answer now," he said determinedly.

"I don't know what question you mean," she pouted. "You have asked me a dozen."

"You do know what question I mean; but I can ask it again if you wish. Wynema, I love you and want you for my little wife. Will you marry me?" he asked, nervously flushing but very earnest.

The girl glanced up half-smiling, saying:

"Robin what would our parents say? Would your mother accept a little black Indian for a daughter?"

"My sweetheart must not call herself names," replied Robin, throwing his arm about her, evidently to keep her from falling.

"Come and let's tell them all about it, now, and we can soon decide that point."

"No, oh, no!" she exclaimed, shrinking as from a blow. "Promise me, Robin, that you will not tell them until I am gone. I cannot bear to think of them knowing it now."

"Why, darling! I want the world to know it; I am so proud of my little girl;" and he pressed her fondly to him.

"Oh, it isn't that, Robin; but I fear your mother may care, and I should feel criminal to think I had come down here and stolen you away like a wolf steals away a lamb."

"Am I very like a lamb, dear?" Robin asked mischievously to divert her thoughts from so solemn a channel.

"No," she answered; "you are more like a scape-goat; but I should not compare you to either; you are more on the bruin order."

"Aren't you ashamed to talk about your sweetheart so? You must pay me for that;" and he stooped to kiss her lips.

"No, Robin, not now," she said, turning away her head and covering her face. "When we are married," flushing at the word, "will be soon enough."

"But sweetheart, you are going away to-morrow and I won't get to see you for ever so long, perhaps never;" looking very doleful. "Just kiss me once and call me sweetheart and I won't ask you for another for ever so long," he pleaded; but she persistently refused, saying:

"I must go now, Robin. You must not try to keep me longer, for I have so much to do;" and she strove to dismount from her perch, but seeing the unavailableness of striving to keep her against her will, he sprang down, and offering his hands guided her to the ground. When she leapt downward he threw his arms about her and, pressing her to his bosom, kissed her repeatedly. "Good-bye, my own little darling! Good-bye!" he murmured. She drew herself away, crying reproachfully:

"Oh, Robin!" and fled into the house.

An hour or so later when she entered her room she found a note lying on the table addressed to her. Opening it she read:

"MY OWN DARLING: Forgive me. I could not help it, indeed I could not; you were so cruel to refuse me that one little boon when we are so soon to be separated. Don't get angry with me, and I'll promise never, *no never* to be guilty of the same offense again—if I can help it. If you can forgive me smile at me when you come in to tea. Your own, ROBIN."

Wynema read and re-read this note through. There were few words in it and those few very understandable. Still she reperused and kissed the billet and put it safely away. When she went down to supper, arrayed most becomingly, and looking bewitchingly lovely Robin thought—but a lover is always a little partial to his heart's desire—she looked at Robin mischievously, and pouted out her pretty lips so temptingly that no doubt he would have been guilty of the offense for which he was then forgiven, had they been alone.

16

The Return

If Genevieve Weir had doubted the affection which the Indians bestowed upon her, she was fully convinced of its warmth by the welcome home she and Wynema received. Friends and neighbors for miles around had gathered to see them and bid them welcome home, their features portraying the emotion they felt over the safe arrival of the two travelers.

Gerald Keithly and Carl Peterson were there, of course, and the former said to Genevieve when he had an opportunity to speak to her alone:

"I am so glad to see you return, Genevieve, for we have all missed you sadly; and I believe you are not very sorry to be with us again, judging by the light in your eyes. Am I right?"

"Yes," she answered softly, "I am glad to be among a people so appreciative. I know now how my people love me."

"Can you measure my love in the same way, Genevieve? No," he said as she raised her hand to stop him, "Let me speak now. I have been true to my word and never annoyed you in my letters, though it was hard sometimes. Now let me free the love that has been barred up so long. Oh, my darling, I hope you may never know what heart-hunger is!—the yearning for some one to care for you—to care whether you live or die; yes, I know you care in a way,"—in answer to her expression—"but not in the way I want you to—the way you must care. Dear,

65

I feel that God will not deprive me of the boon of your love and life-companionship. But I am tiring you and will not say any more. Promise me, dear, that when you begin to care for me you will let me know. Will you darling?"

"Yes," she answered in almost a whisper; for she thought, "I hope he cannot tell; I wonder if my manner is changed."

They joined the company and the conversation turned on the topic of the day—allotment.

"What do you think of it now, Genevieve?" asked Gerald.

"Just as I have always thought. The question will never be settled in but one way."

"And that is—?"

"And that is, the land will be divided finally; I think there is no doubt of it, for the half-breeds mostly favor it; and there are so many white people in here now that they will urge the measure until it is passed."

"It is a shame that the white people will not leave this little spot of earth alone," said Carl Peterson. "There are those vast plains in Texas and the large states and territories of the west where emigration and population are invited. Why do not these people who are so much in need of homes go there and make them?"

"You are too hard for me, Peterson; unless it be that people have the same feeling about the territory as cattle have for hay when it is well fenced in. You remember the little plot of the old farmer who wanted some stubble eaten by his cows. He had noticed that cows are peculiar animals, desiring what they should not have, and refusing what they should have; so he placed a high fence about the stubble, and the cows, leaving the oats and corn near them, nearly broke their necks getting the stubble, which they devoured with a relish. Thus it is with the white people, I suppose," and he smiled happily, for he felt more joyous than usual that night.

17

Another Visit to Keithly College

"Here is a letter for Wynema. Where is she?" asked Genevieve one day as she came in from the post-office. "Ah, here she is; poring over what? Elaine? How sentimental! But here is your letter, and it seems to me the chirography is familiar to me. Do you and Robin correspond, Wynema?" she asked as she looked closely at the girl.

"Yes," faltered Wynema, flushing under her friend's scrutiny.

"Ah, that accounts for these sentimental sighs and pale cheeks! Is this to be my little sister?" and Genevieve kissed her friend lovingly.

"Yes; do you mind it?" asked Wynema keeping her eyes on the floor.

"Mind it? Oh, you little rogue! Don't you know I am delighted with the idea?" embracing her warmly. "I mind it so much that I shall write to Robin to-night, congratulating him; but he doesn't deserve it, for he is so reticent about the engagement. I wonder why he didn't tell me before I came away."

"I am to blame for that," confessed Wynema. "I would not consent for him to do so, though he desired very much to tell you."

"And why did you wish to keep me in ignorance?" asked Genevieve, curiously.

"Oh, because—because, I feared you might not like it—that the engagement might not please you," faltered the girl.

"But I should have known sooner or later. You would have told me before you married—now don't blush so at the word—Wynema Weir. What a pretty name! Don't you think so?" teasingly.

"Yes, almost as pretty as Genevieve Keithly. I believe I like it better, but I know you don't," said Wynema with her usual spirit.

It was Genevieve's turn to flush and grow confused. "Who told you anything about that?" she asked, in a low tone.

"I have two eyes and two ears and I generally use them when it is honorable to do so. But as for that matter, a half-blind person would know *that*," emphasizing the that. "Why, I knew *that* before we went away."

"You knew what, before we went away?" innocently.

"Why, that Mr. Keithly is partial to you to say the least of it, and that he intended propounding the momentous question; and I didn't think he would 'get the mitten,' " Wynema added mischievously.

"But you know that I was engaged to Maurice before I went home—well not engaged exactly, but it was almost the same as an engagement. I did not think of Mr. Keithly in that way at all, then."

"But you do now, do you?" Wynema laughed; "I knew you would not marry Mr. Mauran as soon as I saw you together. You are too dissimilar. I hope you will not get offended with me for saying so, but I did not particularly like Mr. Mauran, and I do Mr. Keithly. I think you two were made for each other."

"Do you think he loves me, Wynema?" Genevieve asked in a low tone, lowering her eyes.

"Oh, no, not at all!" scornfully. "The most casual observer would know that he is perfectly indifferent toward you," and

the girl ran laughing away, to read her letter alone, leaving
Genevieve to think what she could of what she had said.

"Go to Keithly College! Oh, yes, I shall be delighted to do so.
Let me go and tell Miss Genevieve;" and Wynema left Gerald
Keithly to himself, after seating him comfortably in the sitting
room. Genevieve came in presently, consented to the proposed
visit, and soon they were on their way.

They laughed and chatted for some distance, when they
suddenly became quiet.

"Wynema," asked Gerald presently, "of what are you
thinking?"

"Do you really wish to know?" she asked saucily. "Well it
is this: 'Two souls with but a single thought; two hearts that
beat as one,'" and she looked at him significantly.

"See that pretty squirrel, yonder!" Genevieve exclaimed,
suddenly, her cheeks flushing, but otherwise not seeming to
have heard what was said.

"But that is not a squirrel, though, Mihia," laughed Wynema wickedly. "Squirrels do not peck, do they? and listen—
what a noise that makes!"

Gerald noted his lady-love's confusion with a great throb of
joy; but, pitying her, he changed the subject to one of general
interest, and soon they drove into the College grounds where
teachers and pupils met them, and asked for a description
of their trip. Genevieve motioned to Wynema, who in an
exaggerated, comical manner related everything laughable that
had occurred to them during their visit.

While she was talking Gerald led Genevieve away to see the
plant again—not the beautiful, blooming plant as before. No,
there was nothing interesting about it now; but these foolish
young people bent their heads over it and seemed perfectly
entranced with its beauty.

"Have you anything to say to me now, Genevieve?" Gerald asked; but she only lowered her head. He bent his head to catch her reply, and, failing, added: "You know I asked you to tell me when you felt that you could love me a little, and you promised you would; I thought I would wait for you to come and tell me, but I could not. I am so anxious to know, dear, for my great love makes me impatient."

Genevieve bent her head still lower and whispered:

"Have you forgotten about Maurice Mauran?"

"No," he answered; "but when you came back unmarried, I knew that something must have occurred to separate you—I felt that you would never marry him. And, dear, when you came back alone I felt a great wave of happiness thrill through my being, for I hoped my darling would learn to love me at last. Can you not love me the least bit in the world, Genevieve?" he asked tremulously.

"No, Gerald," she whispered.

"Why, my darling?" disappointedly.

"Because—because—oh, Gerald! Don't you know? Because I love you *more* than *that*," and she gave him one sweet look out of her soft, love-bedewed eyes.

And so Gerald Keithly won his heart's desire.

18

Turmoil with the Indians

"Mother," said Gerald Keithly, some years after the events recorded in the last chapter, one morning as he came in to breakfast, "I notice the Indians living on the reservation in Dakota are in trouble, and I fear, if their requests are not granted, the white settlers will have to suffer for it. I hope there will be no trouble."

"Indeed, yes," replied Mrs. Weir, shuddering. "But what is the cause of the disturbance. I know there must be some serious cause, for the Indians have never gone on the war-path, or even troubled their white neighbors, without abundant cause."

"Hurrah for the little Mith!" cried Genevieve, who had been attending to the wants of little Master Gerald, aged three years, the pet and idol of his mother's heart, and who now turned to take her accustomed place. "She is worse than I am, Gerald, isn't she?" and she smiled lovingly at her husband.

This was a very happy family seated around the breakfast table in the pleasant dining-room of Keithly College. "The little Mith," as she was lovingly called by her children, alias Mrs. Weir, the beloved and respected of all about her, carried on her physiognomy deeper finger-prints of time than formerly; but no one would have thought of calling this gentle, merry-hearted little woman old, for her heart was as fresh and her eyes as bright as in the spring-time of life. And, as for

Gerald and Genevieve, the happy lovers still, the vitalizer, love, only made them younger and handsomer. Opposite Genevieve sat Winnie, the "baby," now a lovely young lady.

"I am sure, Genevieve, I always espoused the cause of the Indians," Mrs. Weir said in answer to her daughter's remark. "For the reason, and that alone, that I felt that they had been mistreated by our race, I allowed you to leave home and come among them—that your life's work might compensate in a measure for what the white people have taken from them."

"And the white people, not being content with other robberies, have even taken the little compensation mother thought to give the Indians," laughed Winnie, mischievously.

"Tell auntie she is too general in her remarks," Gerald senior prompted his hopeful son; "The white *people* did not commit this robbery."

"Well, one of them did anyhow," Winnie replied.

"But that is not answering my question," interrupted Mrs. Weir. "I asked what caused the Indian troubles."

"Here is what the papers say: 'A dispatch from Sisseton, South Dakota, says that the twelve thousand Indians on the Sisseton and Wahpeton reservations are on the verge of starvation at the opening of winter, because of the Government's failure to furnish subsistence. The Interior Department has authorized the expenditure of $2,000 for the relief of the red men, but upon this small sum of money over two thousand men, women and children must live for a period of over six months of rigorous weather. Their chiefs and most able-bodied men have petitioned the Government to send them aid; "for," they say, "if they do not get some help there will be great suffering and actual starvation."'"

"Another paper says, 'the Indians of the Northwest have the Messiah craze and are dancing themselves to death—dancing the ghost dance. They dance all night, and expect to see their

Messiah at dawn.' The editor adds: 'If the United States army would kill a few thousand or so of the dancing Indians there would be no more trouble.'"

"Some one should answer that, Gerald," said Genevieve, indignantly.

"And some one has, dear," quoth Gerald. "Old Masse— Hadjo—comes to the front in this letter. I will read what he says: 'You say if the United States army would kill a few thousand or so of the dancing Indians there would be no more trouble. I judge by the above language that you are a Christian and are disposed to do all in your power to advance the cause of Christ. You are doubtless a worshiper of the white man's Saviour, but are unwilling that the Indians should have a Messiah of their own. The Indians have never taken kindly to the Christian religion as preached and practiced by the whites. Do you know why this is the case? Because the Good Father of all has given us a better religion—a religion that is all good and no bad—a religion that is adapted to our wants. You say if we are good, obey the ten commandments and never sin any more, we may be permitted eventually to sit upon a white rock and sing praises to God forevermore, and look down upon our heathenly fathers, mothers, sisters and brothers in hell. It won't do. The code of morals practiced by the white race will not compare with the morals of the Indians. We pay no lawyers or preachers, but we have not one-tenth part of the crime that you do. If our Messiah does come, we will not try to force you into our belief. We will never burn innocent women at the stake, or pull men to pieces with horses because they refuse to join with us in our ghost dances. You white people had a Messiah, and if history is to be believed, nearly every nation has had one. You had twelve apostles; we have only eleven and some of them are already in the military guard-house. We had also a Virgin Mary, but she is also in the guard-house. You are anxious to get hold of our Messiah so you can put him in irons. This you may do—in fact you may crucify him as you did that other one—but you cannot convert the Indians to the Christian religion until you contaminate them with the blood of the white man. The white man's heaven is repulsive to the Indian nature, and if the white man's hell suits you, keep it. I think there will be white rogues enough to fill it.' He signs himself, 'Your most obedient, Masse Hadjo.' Just think, the poor things are starving to death and are praying to their Messiah to relieve them, as nobody on earth will. And because of this, the white people want them killed."

"Don't you think there will be fighting before it is all over with?" asked Mrs. Weir.

"Yes; I do not think there is any doubt of it, if the United States Army attempts to stop their dancing. Why, hello, Peterson! What's up, that you are out so early?"

"Now, Keithly, you know I am not a sluggard. But enough is the matter to rouse the most Rip-Van-Winkle-like sleeper. My people, the Sioux, are about to go on the war-path. I see they are being driven to it by the treatment of the United States Government and their own agents, who have leagued together to starve and slaughter this defenseless people. Did you see this account of troops being sent out to quell the riot, which larger rations would have rendered unnecessary and impossible? Just think of those poor fellows subsisting on about one cent's worth per day! It may be called an oversight of the Government, but I call it a shame, a crime for which the American people will yet be punished. But I did not come here to say this, for I know you feel as I do about it; but I came for another purpose. I want a vacation, a furlough of indefinite length, for I want to go among these troubled people and do all I can for them."

"Certainly, certainly, my dear fellow! I know just how you feel about it, and I should accompany you if school were not in session. At any rate, I give you Godspeed and will follow you with my prayers;" and Gerald grasped his friend's hand warmly.

"Thank you, my dear kind friend," Carl responded, feelingly.

"But, Mr. Peterson, you might get killed," Winnie said, to change the scene which she said was too masculinely one-sided.

"No, Miss Winnie, I enlist in the Army of the Heavenly General and wear his shield and helmet; therefore I do not fear. He will preserve me to do his work; and if my life-work shall be finished on the Sioux battle-field, then so be it. It will still be His will. But you mistake my errand, Miss Winnie. I am going in peace, to try to effect a peaceful adjustment of these troubles, and I shall not be subjected to the dangers of the battle-field."

"I wonder what Bessie will say?" sighed Winnie, significantly. The young man blushed, and Gerald, sympathizing with his feeling, drew him from the room to talk over matters more thoroughly.

19

The Family Together

"Oh, mamma! auntie Wynema! and bebee!" shouted Gerald junior, or Gerlie as he called himself, who had been playing near a window that overlooked the front part of the house. "And bebee, mamma; tum, 'es do see bebee," and he ran to the door catching the skirts of one entering the room.

Yes, it is Wynema, but Wynema matured—the promise of the bud fulfilled in the rose. Time has only beautified her; for happiness is his antagonist and has gained the mastery. She leads by the hand a little tot of a brown-eyed golden-haired girl, one year Gerlie's junior—the pride and joy of her parents and the idol of her grandparents' hearts.

"Her name shall be Wynema for her mother," Robin had said; but Wynema would not have it so. "Call it Genevieve for the dearest friend I ever had;" and so she was named.

But various were this little lady's sobriquets. She was "Angel," "Pet," "Love," and "Darling," to mamma, and "Dada," "Sweetheart" and "Duchess," to auntie and uncle; "Bebee," to Gerlie, and all the pet names in the Indian vocabulary, to "Damma" and "Dampa."

After greetings had been exchanged and the visitors made comfortable, Genevieve spoke of the Indian troubles in the Northwest, and Carl Peterson's proposed journey.

"I think he is right," quoth Wynema; "and I know Robin would like to go if it were possible. I should like to go myself if I could be of any service; but I should only be a hindrance. Robin showed me an extract from one of our great dailies, which states the death of Sitting Bull, the Sioux chief, and relates how it occurred. It was reported to the Indian police that Sitting Bull proposed starting to the Bad Lands; so they started out at once, followed by a troop of cavalry under Capt. Fouchet, and infantry under Col. Drum to arrest him and bring him back. When the police reached Sitting Bull's camp they found him making preparations for departure. So they immediately arrested him and started back. His followers tried to retake him, and in the effort, he, his son and six of his men were killed, as well as five of the police. Poor fellows! They are starved almost to death, and in the attempt to crawl off to themselves are caught and slaughtered like cattle. It is a shame!"

"Ah, indeed a great crime, for which my people will be made to answer," sighed Mrs. Weir.

"They would not have to answer for it if they were all as sensible and human as you are 'little Mith,'" answered Wynema, lovingly. "But I must tell you about the school, which I neglected to do, in thinking and talking of this other matter. We now have two hundred pupils and applications for fifty more, but we haven't the room. Robin says the Council will enlarge the building next year, so we can accommodate a still larger number. He is as enthusiastic over educating the Indians as I am, and sometimes I tell him he is more so. And Bessie is the same way. I tell her she will be running away with one of our warriors; but I rather think she prefers one of your pale-faces."

"Do you mean, Carl?" questioned Genevieve.

"Yes, and I do most sincerely hope so," Wynema answered. "I left her below stairs, in the garden talking with him and

Gerald; but I don't suppose Gerald burdened them with his company long."

"No, he understands all about that," laughed Genevieve. "See how well the babies play together. Don't kiss sweetheart so much, Gerlie; you worry her. She doesn't want to be kissed away; do you, Duchess? Come right here to your auntie."

But instead the child hid her face against her mother, holding one tiny hand to ward off Gerlie's caresses.

"You won't object to kisses so much after awhile, Duchess; when you are older you will rather like to be caressed," said Winnie shaking her head with mock gravity at her little niece.

"Ask Aunt Winnie if she knows from experience," Wynema prompted, teasingly.

"Yes, others' experience. I notice you and Genevieve were not averse to it, and cannot get enough of kissing, even now," answered Winnie saucily, delighting to tease even her best friends.

"I wonder if Dr. Bradford would not give an opinion in favor of osculation if Winnie asked for it," remarked Genevieve slyly. "Wynema, you have no idea of the energy that young man possesses. He is positively riding all day long and sometimes all night, visiting his patients, yet he finds it convenient to drop in here about every other night in the week."

"Is that so?" asked Wynema, prolonging each word, as if in great surprise, her eyes sparkling merrily. "You must have a deal of sickness here," innocently.

"Well, he has one patient, suffering with heart disease whom he seems to think needs much attention and—"

"Now, sister, you know he comes to see Gerald or Mr. Peterson on business," interrupted Winnie, flushing.

"Strange, he stays after business is dismissed, and directs so much of his conversation to—well not to me—and as for his eyes—well, I won't say any more; but I can't believe he looks at Gerald *all* the time," and Genevieve caught up baby Gerlie and waltzed him over the floor.

"Now, girls, you must not tease my baby so much," said Mrs. Weir, looking lovingly at the three, "for I do want, and have always wanted, an M. D. in our family, and I shan't object to her Winning Dr. Bradford at all."

"Now, mother, no punning," laughed the girls; and all went on as merry as a marriage bell.

20

Among the Rebels

In a tepee, a hostile tent, stood our friend, Carl Peterson, surrounded by the chiefs of tribes with whom he was in deep consultation regarding the Indian troubles. By his side stood Robin Weir who had insisted that it would be dangerous for Peterson to go alone, though Carl laughed at the idea. The Indians dressed in their savage costumes, with war-paint and feathers in abundance, stood with lowered, determined brows, attentively listening to what their friend was saying.

"Go into the reservation and surrender your fire-arms, friends," he said. "Place yourselves in a submissive attitude, and the Government will protect you; you will not be starved again, for those criminal agents have been discharged and better ones employed."

"But," remonstrated the dark Wildfire, "what assurance have we that these agents will treat us better than the others? We were once a large and powerful nation, ruling over a vast portion of this country of yours. By the white man's cruelty and treachery we have been driven farther and farther away, until we now occupy this Government reservation, in a climate so cold and exposed to such hardships that our numbers have diminished until we are but a handful—a mere speck of what we were. In the old days we were free; we hunted and fished as we pleased, while our squaws tilled the soil. Now we are driven to a small spot, chosen by the pale-faces, where we are watched over and controlled by agents who can starve us to death at their will. Think you, I can hear of peace when I see my noble companions slain because they refuse to obey the commands of the military men? When our squaws and children are shot down like dogs before our eyes? May the Great Father hear me when I say, let this arm wither, let these eyes grow dim, let this savage heart still its beating, when I stand still and make peace with a Government whose only policy is to exterminate my race." His dark eyes dilated, his stalwart frame shook, and his whole attitude and expression betokened the greatest determination and earnestness.

"But, my dear friend Wildfire," said Carl Peterson laying his hand on the Indian's shoulder, "this is not a policy to live by."

"Then let it be a policy to *die* by," defiantly spoke the Indian. "If we cannot be free, let us die. What is life to a caged bird, threatened with death on all sides? The cat springs to catch it and hangs to the cage looking with greedy eyes at the victim. Strange, free birds gather round its prison and peck at its eyes, taunting it with its captivity until it beats its wings against the cage and longs for freedom, yea, even the freedom of *death*. So it is with us. The white man has caged us, here, for his greedy brothers to devour. Do you know that one of our chiefs, Few Tails, with a few of his followers, went on a hunt the other day, and when returning, a party of pale-face, cowardly cowboys met and killed them all but Few Tails' wife who was wounded until she will die? Great Eye and I were coming back from a consultation of our chiefs when we found her wounded and dying on the roadside, with no one near. She could barely tell what had occurred; but we saw the bodies of the slaughtered braves about three hundred yards away, and they told their own story. Yes, those bleeding, gaping wounds those eyes glaring in death, those stiff bodies lying where they

willing to go to-day and surrender my arms, if my friends will go; and, if not, I shall go soon and take the old men, the women and children."

The others then expressed themselves—the older chiefs agreeing with Great Eye, the younger ones with Wildfire, who stood with folded arms and lowered brows, saying: "Cowards alone surrender."

"We will not quarrel with you, my brother," said Great Eye, calmly; "for I pray that you may not have to surrender to a far greater and more powerful sovereign than the United States Government—that Great Commander to whom we all must, sooner or later, lay down our arms—Death. Good-bye, brothers, fare-thee-well. What are you going to do my friend, Carl Peterson? the hostile tent is no place for you. Your pale-face brothers in yonder camp may misunderstand your motives and slay you. You had better go with me to the reservation."

"No," answered Carl, sadly. "I came to cast my lot among your misguided and mistreated people, to do all I can for them, toward reconciling them to my people and to the Government. I came by the military camp and informed the commander of my object, and he let me pass. I shall not be harmed."

"Did he, the great pale-face soldier, send you to make peace with us?" Wildfire asked, proudly drawing himself up.

"No, the Great Father, the God of Peace sent me," Carl said reverently. "I worked among you many years preaching to and teaching your people. I hoped I might, for this reason, have some influence over you. I hoped to win you over to the side of right; but I have failed," Carl answered sadly.

"My friend Carl Peterson, I would give you my right arm if I could; I would help you in any way I could; but give up my liberty, *never*, no, not to my mother."

"That is just what I could never ask you to do, Wildfire," Carl answered cautiously, seeing his advantage. "If you do as you are now determined to do, you will lose your life; but if—as I hope and pray you may do—you return to the reservation, you will have all the liberty your treaty allows. The general assured me you should have your fire-arms to use in hunting whenever you wish; you have only to apply to him for them. He will tell you all about that when you go back. Believe me, my friend, it will be best. I love you and I don't want to see you lose your life, as I know you will do if you still persist in your determination to resist the Government. Can you not see that you would be crushed as a bird in the paws of a lion? for you are but a handful and the Government is mighty. You have a wife and children. Do you want to see them slaughtered as Few Tails and his, and his band were? Take them to the reservation and make peace, and there will then be no danger of that."

"Don't persuade me any more," the Indian replied, heaving a great sigh. "I would do as you advise if I could, but I cannot. I should be in the gall of bitterness if I dwelt on the reservation after this, and I prefer to die than be so miserable. My wife and children shall go into the reservation with the other women and children; and I—perhaps, the Great Father above is looking down and sees how his poor, untutored, defenseless savages are treated by their wiser brothers, and will arm me with strength and courage to battle for my oppressed people. You speak of my wife and children. Ah, well you may. It is for them I resist, for them I shall battle, and for them I shall die, if need be—that my sons may not grow up the oppressed wards of a mighty nation—the paltry beggars to whom the pitiful sum of one cent is doled out, when the whole vast country is theirs by right of inheritance. Tell me, you who are wiser—are learned in the arts and sciences of all times—tell me, is it *right* for one nation to drive another off and usurp their land, take away their money, and even their liberty? Say, is it right? Ah, you cannot answer, for you dare not answer, yes. And again; is it right for the nation who have been trampled upon, whose land, whose property, whose liberty, whose everything but life, have been taken away, to meekly submit and still bow their heads for the yoke? Why the very ox has more spirit than that. Beat him and see if he readily submits to the yoke. No, no, my friend. You are kind, and you mean well, but you can never understand these things as I do. You have never been oppressed. The worm much trampled upon will finally turn and defend itself even if it die in the attempt. Ah, you are grieved; I am sorry. I would that I could do as you desire, but I cannot. Pray to your Father that He look mercifully down on His poor savages and guide them out of their troubles; that they may have the liberty above they will never enjoy here."

Carl knelt among his Indian friends and lifted his voice, full of tears, in earnest, fervent supplication to the "All-Father;" that He look mercifully down and soften the hearts of this misguided people, speak into their hearts the "peace that passeth all understanding," and guide them into the path that leads to life and liberty everlasting. At the close of his prayer he repeated the prayer taught by the "Prince of Peace," which he had translated into the Sioux language, and the Indians with one accord joined with him and closed with a fervent "Amen." Carl noticed that they were all much touched, and Wildfire's eyes were moist with feeling.

"Carl Peterson," he said, "I may never see you again on earth. Take this belt my mother made for me when I was a boy; I have treasured it because she wrought it; it was her hands that fashioned it, that wove the beads in and out in curious device, and with her own hands she used to fasten it about my waist. Take it and as often as you look at it think of Wildfire, the rebellious, defiant savage; but think he would not have grieved his best friend, if he had not been driven to do so by the cruelty and oppression of the white man." With these and other words he bade his friend Godspeed.

"I will not urge you more, now, Wildfire; but I shall pray for you continually and shall ask the Father of Peace to rule in your breast. Remember what I say now—it comes from the Bible you love to hear so well. *God* says these words: 'Vengeance is mine, saith the Lord, I will repay.' I shall come to see you again for I shall not leave your country until peace is made." So saying, he warmly shook the Indian's hands and left the tent, attended by his friend.

Wildfire and his followers were graver than before this conversation took place, but they were not in the least shaken in their purpose. They, as well as all their Indian friends, made ready for the departure of the infirm, the women and children, and many of their warriors who had determined to enter the reservation. Wildfire's wife, the fair Miscona, clung to her husband with the tenderness of despair.

"If I go, if I leave you, I shall never see you again," she cried. "I know you have called up your warriors; that you have planned a battle; that you will try to surround the pale-faces and kill them; but, oh, my husband, do you not know they are more powerful than you? You are strong and brave, and if you had half the number the white man has you could blot them out; but you have only a few brave men, and they are so many. And, if you were to succeed in killing these, don't you know the great Government has thousands more it would send out to kill you? Oh, Wildfire, my dear husband, go with me to the reservation. Here we can live happily and peacefully with our children and among our people. If you stay here you will be killed, and what happiness could your devoted wife ever expect to have? When I left my father's tepee to go with you, you promised to love me and take care of me always;

but you will not be fulfilling your promise if you leave me to make my way to the reservation while you remain here," and she clung to him praying and beseeching in vain. All that she could get him to promise was that he would take her to the reservation, which promise lightened her heart considerably, for she hoped to allure him in and keep him if once she got him there. Ah Miscona! Little you knew that the fountain once stirred from its depths can never be quieted.

21

Civilization or Savage Barbarity

A dark figure with a babe in her arms creeps stealthily from a tent into the dark night. Softly and stealthily it steps until it reaches the outskirts of the reservation, where it is met by other dark figures, some with the papoose, some without. When these figures are out of hearing distance, they run rapidly and joyously toward the tepees of the defiant Indians. Sixteen miles! Ah, that is nothing to one going on a mission of love. Patriotism has inspired men to greater deeds. Paul Revere and Philip Sheridan have been made famous for a terrible ride; these dark figures, running, sliding and falling along the dark road in the bitter night, will not be known to the world, for theirs was only a walk for love. They reached the tents of the rebels.

"Miscona," exclaimed her husband reproachfully, hardly believing his eyes. "And the papoose! You must go back, Miscona. It is not safe here," said he throwing his arms about them. "We are to battle to-morrow. Yes, to-morrow's sun, when he opens his great eye, will see the rebel band of Indians surrounding their white tyrants, and before he closes it the ground will be strewn with the dead bodies of our enemies, or of us. We have arranged our skirmish so that it will seem at first that our numbers are smaller than they are. Then when the enemy engages this brave few, the others will rush up from all sides, with a mighty whoop, and surround them. This is our plan; whether it is a good one remains to be proved. How many women came with you?"

"About forty, and many of them carried the papoose."

"Well, you must start back to-morrow. It will be dangerous for you to remain here."

But "man proposes and God disposes,"—in this instance, the Indian proposes, the Government disposes. It was reported by scouts sent out for that purpose, to the commander of the troops stationed on the reservation, that the Indians were plotting war and were planning to surround them on the following day. So the general sent a detachment to meet the "hostiles," and surprise them, and to capture all unharmed if possible. But, instead of this, the Indians were slaughtered like cattle, shot down like dogs. Surprised at the sudden apparition of white soldiers drawn up in line of battle, when they supposed the soldiers to be in their camps miles distant, their presence of mind deserted them, and it was with difficulty that Wildfire rallied his forces. To add to this consternation, on turning about toward his camps, he beheld the women who had followed them to battle, instead of going to the reservation as they had promised and started to do. It was useless to motion them back, for on they came, their faces speaking with noiseless eloquence. "We have lived with you; we will die with you." Up they rushed into the line of battle where they more unfitted the men for fighting.

"Good and gracious Father, Miscona! You have lost the battle for me," groaned the chieftain.

"It is a lost cause. You will die and I will die by your side, my husband," she replied resolutely.

Then came the dust and smoke and din of battle, the hurrying forward of the foes to the onset.

"Indians, I command you to go into the reservation quietly

or, by God, you die here in your tracks!" shouted the commander.

"We shall die, then," shouted Wildfire in return; "but we will never enter the reservation alive!"

Oh! the terrible, terrible battle! Old Chikena in giving the circumstances relating to it to Wynema, always closed her eyes and shuddered. Everywhere could be seen Wildfire fighting and urging his troops on, and everywhere, the iron-clad hand of the white soldiers beating down his Indian adversary—yes, and not only the men, but the helpless, defenseless women and children. The command was, "No quarter! Kill them every one."

In the midst of the one-sided battle, Wildfire was slain, felled to the ground, and by his side, as was afterwards found, his devoted Miscona—only an Indian squaw, so it did not matter.

The Indians, seeing their leader slain, fled precipitately to the camps, followed for some distance by their adversaries, who finally drew up in line and marched back to quarters. On the night following the battle came a terrible blizzard—wind so piercingly cold that it freezes the very marrow in the bones of one so unfortunate as to be exposed to it. Out on the battle-field, with no covering but the open sky lay the bodies of the dying and dead Indians, left there by friends and foes. Over here are the bodies of Wildfire and Miscona, free at last, and the little papoose sweetly sleeping between them. Over there lies a warrior, groaning and murmuring—and everywhere is blood, blood! Over everything, around everything, on everything. Oh! the awful sight!

A dark form is seen presently gliding among them administering to the wants of the dying as best she can. It is an Indian squaw, watching over the battle-field, guarding the dead and dying. Like Rizpah of old, on the Gibeah plain, she took her distant station and watched to see that nothing came near to harm her beloved dead.

During the forenoon of the following day, two men rode on the ghastly scene, astonished at the almost numberless dead and wounded bodies strewn over the plain; astonished to see women and children slain among the number, for it has ever been the policy of a strong, brave nation to protect the helpless, the weak, the defenseless.

Alighting and walking among the dead, they saw what at first they had not noticed, the form of the Indian woman kneeling among the wounded. Carl Peterson walked up to where she knelt and addressed her.

"Woman, why are you here, and whence did you come?"

She raised her head mournfully, her face dripping with tears, and started as she recognized the speaker; "Carl Peterson!" she exclaimed.

"Yes, and is this Chikena, the happy wife of the brave Great Wind, when I last saw her?" he asked. "What are you doing on this field of battle?"

"Ah! The times have changed for poor Chikena," she answered, weeping. "Here lies the dead body of the brave Great Wind, and yonder lies his son. Dead! Dead! I am all alone in the world—the only one left of my tribe. Why did not the Great Father take me too?"

"How long have you been here, poor soul?" Carl asked sympathetically. "And have you been here all alone?"

"Yes, all alone since they left me with my dead. The pale-faces killed our brave Wildfire and his beautiful Miscona— yonder they lie in each other's arms—and then our people fled back to their tents, the soldiers pursuing until they reached the creek. I did not leave, for I did not care what became of me—my loved ones were gone and I staid to protect them. But, oh, the bitter, bitter night! The cold wind swept by me and tortured me with its keen, freezing breath; but I drew my blanket more closely about me and defiantly watched my dead.

The wolves came to take them but I lighted a fire and kept the wolves at bay. Then the wounded groaned with their wounds and the cold, and I dragged as many of them together as I could and covered them with my blanket. Then, uncovered, in the bitter cold, how I walked and heaped the fire higher and longed for the coming of day! When day broke I went about among the dead, washed their wounds and ministered to their wants as I could; and so I have been doing since. On my rounds I found three little papooses, about three months old, all wrapped up snugly in their dead mothers' bosoms. I took them, wrapped them in the blankets of the ones they will never know, and yonder they lie, sleeping sweetly."

Carl went to the tents of the Indians, informed them concerning the state of affairs, gathered together wagons for the dead and stretchers for the dying and wounded, and repaired to the scene we had just quitted. There the Indians gathered together their dead and buried them, and took the wounded back to their tents.

The two friends with Chikena and the babies returned to the reservation, there to await the termination of the Indian war of the Northwest.

With a few slight skirmishes, the papers say, only the death of a few "Indian bucks," the war of the Northwest ended.

"But," you ask, my reader, "did not the white people undergo any privations? Did not the United States army lose two brave commanders and a number of privates?" Oh, yes. So the papers tell us; but I am not relating the brave (?) deeds of the white soldier. They are already flashed over the world by electricity; great writers have burned the midnight oil telling their story to the world. It is not my province to show how brave it was for a great, strong nation to quell a riot caused by the dancing of a few 'bucks' — for *civilized* soldiers to slaughter indiscriminately, Indian women and children. Doubtless it was brave, for so public opinion tells us, and it cannot err. But what will the annals of history handed down to future generations disclose to them? Will history term the treatment of the Indians by the United States Government, right and honorable? Ah, but that does not affect my story! It is the Indian's story—his chapter of wrongs and oppression.

22

Is This Right?

"Wynema, this is a friend of ours whom we found in the Sioux country. Can you speak the language? If so, she will tell you all, and I should like for you to interpret for my benefit. Ask her to tell you about the 'starving time,' as the Indians call the time when they lived on one cent per day," said Robin one day, some weeks after his return home. He had been to Keithly College and had brought Chikena home with him that she might see the "squaw and papoose," as he laughingly called Wynema and Genevieve.

"Very well dear," Wynema replied. "I learned to speak the Sioux language when quite a child. We had an old Sioux woman who lived with us until I was almost grown, when she died. And thus I became familiar with the language."

Then Wynema took the old woman's hand and kissed her softly, remembering the dear ones she had left behind in the burying-ground of the battle-field; and she spoke words of sympathy, leading her to talk of her troubles.

"My husband wishes to hear of your sufferings during the time you came near starving, before the Indian war. Can you tell me while I interpret?"

This is the story she told Wynema and Robin as they sat by the window of the pleasant sitting-room of Hope Seminary.

"There was a time when my people had plenty of land, plenty of cattle and plenty of everything; but after awhile the pale-faces came along, and by partly buying, partly seizing our lands by force, drove us very far away from our fertile country, until the Government placed us on a reservation in the Northwest, where the cold wind sweeps away our tents and almost freezes us. Then the great and powerful Government promised us to supply us with bountiful rations, in return for our lands it had taken. It was the treaty with us. But one day the agent told us the Government was poor, very poor, and could not afford to feed us so bountifully as in the past. So he gave us smaller rations than before, and every day the portion of each grew smaller, until we felt that we were being starved; for our crops failed and we were entirely dependent on the Government rations. Then came the days when one cent's worth daily was issued to each of us. How we all sickened and grew weak with hunger! I saw my boy, my Horda, growing paler and weaker every day, and I gave him my portion, keeping him in ignorance of it, for he would not have taken it had he known. Our chiefs and warriors gathered around the medicine man and prayed him to ask the Great Father what we should do to avert this evil. So the medicine man prayed to the Great Father all night, in his strange, murmuring way; and the next morning he told us to gather together and dance the holy dance to the Great Father and to sing while we danced, 'Great Father, help us! By thy strong arm aid us! Of thy great bounty give us that we may not die.' We were to dance thus until dawn, when the Messiah would come and deliver us. Many of our men died dancing, for they had become so weak from fasting that they could not stand the exertion. Then the great Government heard of our dances, and fearing trouble, sent out troops to stop us."

"Strange the great Government did not hear of your starving too, and send troops to stop *that*," remarked Robin, per parenthesis.

"Then our great chief, Sitting Bull, told us the Government would starve us if we remained on the reservation; but if we would follow him, he would lead us to a country teeming with game, and where we could hunt and fish at our pleasure. We followed him to the Bad Lands where we struck tents, as we were tired, intending to resume our march after we had rested. But one day we saw a cloud of dust, and there rode up a crowd of Indian police with Buffalo Bill at their head. They called out our chief and ordered him to surrender, then arrested him. Sitting Bull fired several shots, instructed his men how to proceed to recapture him, but all to no avail, for the police were backed by the pale-faced soldiers; and they killed our chief, his son, and six of the bravest warriors. Thus began the war of which your husband has already told you. It ended in Indian submission—yes, a submission extorted by blood."

"Buffalo Bill is the assumed name of the man who went about everywhere, taking a crowd of Indians with him and showing them, is he not?" asked Wynema of her husband.

"Yes, he was at the exposition at New Orleans with a band of Indians whom he was then 'showing,' and thus gaining means for subsistence for himself."

"It is strange he would lead a police force against the people who have helped him to gain a livelihood. Do you suppose the Indians who traveled with him became wealthy thereby?" ironically.

"Oh, yes. Very," he answered in the same tone. "Some of the Indians went from near us, and when they came back their friends and neighbors had to make up a 'pony purse' to give them a start. One trip with this 'brave' man was sufficient, though I never heard one of them express a desire to go again."

"There is an old man in the Territory, now, if he has not died recently, who traveled a great deal with Buffalo Bill, and I have never heard anything of the fortune he made. He is old and poor, and goes about doing what odd jobs he can get to do, and his friends almost entirely maintain him. It seems to me that gratitude, alone, to this benighted people who have served him would have rendered him at least *neutral*. If I could not have been for them, I most certainly would not have taken so prominent a part against them," Wynema said indignantly.

"Robin, there was such a scathing criticism of the part the United States Government has taken against the Indians of the Northwest, in the *St. Louis Republic*. I put the paper away to show you, but it has gotten misplaced. The substance of the article was this: the writer commended the Government on its slaughter of the Indians, and recommended that the dead bodies of the savages be used for fertilizers instead of the costly guano Mr. Blaine had been importing. He said the Indians alive were troublesome and expensive, for they would persist in getting hungry and cold; but the Indians slaughtered would be useful, for besides using their carcasses for fertilizers, the land they are now occupying could then be given as homes to the 'homeless whites.' I don't believe I ever read a more sarcastic, ironical article in any newspaper. I should like to shake hands with the writer, for I see he is a just, unprejudiced, thinking man, who believes in doing justice even to an Indian 'buck.' But here are more papers with dots from the battle-field; yet you know more and better about this than the writers of these articles, for you were all around and among the Indians, as well as the soldiers."

"Yes; but I should like to read their story and know their opinion. Good!" said he, reading; "Hear this from the *Cherokee Telephone* and interpret, for Chikena can understand:"

"The papers of the states are discussing the Indian war in the Northwest, its causes, etc. Here is what the matter is in a nutshell: Congress, the Secretary of the Interior, the Army and the Indian agents, have vied with each other in shameful dealings with these poor creatures of the plains. They buy their lands — for half price — make treaties and compacts with them in regard to pay, provisions, etc., then studiously turn and commence to lay plans to evade their promises and hold back their money to squander, and withhold the provisions agreed to be furnished. It must be remembered that these Indians buy, aye, more than pay for all the United States Government lets them have — they have given the Government an acre of land for every pound of beef, sugar, coffee and flour they have ever received. The Government has neglected to comply with treaties with these people — hence the war. They would rather die by the sword and bullet than to see their wives and children perish by degrees. Remember, too, that for every acre of land the United States Government holds to-day, which it acquired from the Indians of any tribe, from the landing of Columbus, it has not paid five cents on an average. The Government owes the Indians of North America justly to-day, ten times more than it will ever pay them. Search history and you will find that these are facts and figures and not mere sentimentalism. Newspaper editors in the states, who speak so vainly of the kindness of the Government to the Indians of this country, should post themselves a little, and each and every one could write a page of history on the United States Government's treatment of the Indians, as black and damnable as hell itself,"

"Phew! That's pretty strong isn't it?" said Robin, finishing and looking up.

"What does Chikena say?"

"She says it is all so. I am glad the editors of newspapers are denouncing the right parties."

23

The Papoose

"When are you coming to Keithly College, to see the papoose?" Carl asked Chikena one day, as the family had all collected in the pleasant parlor of Hope Seminary. He sat beside the old woman, talking cheerfully to her and interpreting bits of the conversation calculated to interest her.

"Not yet," she replied. "I love Wynema, for she seems like my own people to me. You are all very kind to me, but you are not Indian. We are coming to see the papoose, for Wynema wants one for her own."

"Yes? Gerald Keithly wants one, and I shall keep one, and if she wishes she may have one," he answered in a lower tone, for he did not care to be teased; but he reckoned without his host, for Wynema's ears were open toward them.

"What do you propose to do with a three-months-old-papoose, Carl?" she asked mischievously.

"Raise it, if God permits," he answered gravely, but a red flush mounted his brow.

"I'd like to see you in bachelor's quarters, caring for a baby," she laughed; "but I do not expect to do so. Still, if contrary to my expectation, you should happen to raise this papoose, 'single-handed and alone,' and prove successful, I shall like to pass over my charge to you," and so they went on conversing merrily in the Sioux language, that Chikena might not feel neglected among them.

Meanwhile, Gerald, Robin and Genevieve are conversing on graver matters. Winnie has gone in search of Bessie, who went to take the girls walking, and the children are playing quietly in a corner of the room.

"What did you do with the three babies, Mihia?" asked Wynema, presently.

"Gerald didn't think it best to bring them out to-day, so I left them with old Rachel, our Indian nurse, until this afternoon. They are growing rapidly and are as 'cute' and smart as can be. Gerlie wants to nurse and play with them all the time; but there would not be much of them left if I allowed him to, for he would 'love' them to death. See how he is kissing and loving 'Bebee,' now. Let her alone Gerlie, you will make her cry," and she caught up her little namesake, almost smothering her with kisses.

"Come here and show Uncle Rob how you ride a horse," Robin called to the boy, who was pouting disconsolately in a corner; and at the summons he ran gleefully and sat astride of his uncle's foot, laughing merrily as he was tossed into the air.

"Robin, did you see what the papers say about the close of the Northwest war?" asked Gerald, who had been an amused spectator of what had been occurring.

"No," said Robin stopping to listen and get his breath. "I haven't had much time to read up on it. What do they say?"

"Some of the papers think the white soldiers were courage incarnate, and the Indians, dangerous brutes, who should have been slaughtered with the greatest dispatch. This editor differs from the others in this opinion, however. Here is what he says:

"The great Indian war is over—nothing was done except what was intended to be done to start out with. A lot of defenseless Indians were murdered; the Indian agents and contractors reaped a rich harvest; that's all. 'Tis said but true."

"I think that editor is rather bitter," quoth Genevieve.

"Yes, dear," answered Robin; "but if you had seen the Indians slain on the battle-field as we did, and could have heard the groans of the wounded you would not think so."

"But is what this editor says literally so? Do you suppose the United States Government intended things to turn out as they have?"

"We cannot judge of a person's or body's intentions, but from the results of their actions. 'By their fruits ye shall know them,' says God's word; and so we judge by the results that Congress and the Indian agents evidently meant war from the beginning. Because the President favored the capture of Sitting Bull, dead or alive—'but it is preferable to kill him for he is the cause of the Indian troubles'—we judge that he meant to have him slain from the first. That is easy enough to understand. The killing of Sitting Bull was the beginning of hostilities, as could have been foreseen and foreknown. Oh!" he added, placing his hands over his eyes; "I shall never forget that battle-field all strewn with dead and dying men and women and children, and the three little babies resting sweetly and unconsciously in their dead mothers' bosoms. Then the day of the skirmish, the 29th of December, when the soldiers tried to force the Indians to give up their fire-arms and they would not. Wildfire had said to Carl, who had been endeavoring to persuade him to submit quietly: 'I will never surrender my arms and my followers shall not. They are ours to use for our pleasure, or defense if need be. How do we know that when the pale-faces have taken away our fire-arms they will not open fire upon us and kill us because we are defenseless? It is like the cowards who came into our tents and killed our leader and some of our brave warriors, thinking that because our bravest were slain we would then submit to any cruelty to which they might wish to subject us. But *never, never*, so long as Wildfire and his band of braves are spared, shall our squaws and children be starved or slaughtered, before our eyes.' When the soldiers attempted to disarm Wildfire and his followers they opened fire, which was promptly returned and several of Wildfire's followers slain, but he himself escaped to engage in a fiercer conflict.

"The question that keeps urging itself before my eyes is—is all this right, this treatment of the Indians, this non-fulfillment of treaties, this slaughter of a defenseless people, living in the light of wards of the Government? Can it be right for the strong to oppress the weak, the wise to slay the ignorant?"

"I often think with a shudder," remarked Carl Peterson, looking soberly toward Bessie and Winnie, who had just entered and were attentively listening, "of the terrible retribution in store for our Government on account of its treachery and cruelty to the Indians. Wrong is always punished. 'Vengeance is mine, saith the Lord, I will repay.' I am happy to know that all my race are not prejudiced against the Indians; it makes me glad to read the favorite opinion of some of them concerning the poor red brothers. Yet, surely will the hand of the Lord be laid heavily upon the United States Government. It will surely be visited with troubles and sorrows and afflictions, as it has afflicted and troubled the poor, untutored savage. There will be wars and pestilence, anarchies and open rebellions. The subjects of the Government will rise up in defiance of the 'authorities that be.' Oh, it will be trouble—trouble! Let us pray, my brothers and sisters, that God will open the eyes of the Congress and people of the United States that they change their conduct toward the despised red race, and thus avert the evil sure to come upon us if they persist in their present treatment of the Indians."

24

Conclusion

And what became of Bessie and Winnie? Ah, you can guess already! Bessie, of course, married her true knight, Carl Peterson, who abandoned the school-room for the pulpit, throwing his whole soul and life into his work.

The church at Wynema prospered more and more, advancing with the town which is rapidly becoming a city. Other churches of different denominations were built in the place, the people extending a welcome to all churches of God, to build in their midst. Railroads and telegraphs were also welcomed, as the Indians are always pleased with progress in the right direction.

Yes, and Winnie got her M. D. and was finally cured of the heart disease, though she declares she never had it before she knew the doctor.

There, nestled close together, dwelt the happy families of brothers and sisters, growing up happily and prosperously.

Old Chikena dwelt with them till she died, and long after her death were treasured the words she said on the "border-land." Opening her eyes and looking far away, she exclaimed:

"I see the prosperous, happy land of the Indians. Ah, Sitting Bull, beloved chief, it is the land to which you promised to lead us. There, wandering through the cool forests or beside the running streams we may rest our wearied bodies and feast our hungry souls. Farewell! Wynema, thou child of the forest, make haste and seek with me the happy hunting-grounds of our fathers, for not many years of oppression can your people stand. Not many years will elapse until the Indian will be a people of the past. Ah, my people! My people! God gives us rest and peace!"

And the Indian babes found on the Sioux battle-field? Permit us a glance into the future and we shall tell you.

They grew up and prospered in the schools and colleges around them. Miscona, the papoose of the dead chieftain Wildfire, became a famous musician and a wise woman. The others were boys, named respectively, Methven Keithly and Clark Peterson, taking their surnames from their foster-fathers. Methven Keithly became an earnest Christian worker and entered the vineyard of the Lord where it seems barest of fruits—doing missionary work among the so-called wild tribes. Clark Peterson, no less zealous in good deeds however, turned his attentions to the practice of medicine, doing missionary work also; for he taught his people how to preserve their health—a lesson they badly needed. And the Indians—Chikena's dying prophecy—

But why prolong this book into the future, when the present is so fair? The seer withdraws her gaze and looks once more on the happy families nestling in the villages, near together. There they are, the Caucasian and American, the white and the Indian; and not the meanest, not the most ignorant, not the despised; but the intelligent, happy, beloved wife is

WYNEMA, A CHILD OF THE FOREST.

NOTES TO THE TEXT

Title page. "*must* win." From stanza 18 of "The Right Must Win," by British hymn-writer and theologian Frederick William Faber (1814–63).

1. tepees . . . village of tents. Callahan's description is more romantic than accurate. After Removal, the first dwellings the Muscogees constructed were made of upright posts covered with deerskins and elm bark, daubed with mud. Although by the 1880s some of these were still used, houses were more commonly windowless cabins. A few were made of hewn logs (Debo 109, 302).

1. no churches and school-houses. The Muscogees had opposed the establishment of churches in their territory for many years. Though the chiefs in council imposed a penalty of fifty or one hundred lashes on those attending Christian services, by 1842 their opposition had waned. Three years later, Methodist missionaries openly worked in the Muscogee Nation. By 1848, when official opposition ended, the Methodists counted 592 members, 524 of whom were Indian. Two additional boarding schools run by Presbyterians and Methodists were opened in 1847. Boarding schools were primarily attended by mixed bloods. Most of the Methodist and Baptist churches were served by native preachers in 1853 (Debo 116–21).

1. "law unto himself." I am unable to identify this quotation. Daniel F. Littlefield Jr. suggests that it was a common anti-Indian expression used in the late nineteenth century by whites in Oklahoma.

1. "ignorance is bliss." Thomas Gray (1716–71), "Ode on a Distant Prospect of Eton College," line 99.

2. "*every* creature." Mark 16.15.

11. sofke. *Sofke* or *sofkey* was the most important Muscogee food. Beaten corn and water were mixed to form a gruel thin enough to drink, which was left two or three days to sour. A bowl of sofke would be set near the door of each Muscogee home to be offered to visitors (Speck 109; Debo 303).

11. soup . . . made of corn and dried beef. *Wakv Pesb Sakonepke* (beef and corn soup). *Sakonepke* was usually made with corn and pork. Information provided by Alan Cook, historic preservation officer, and Tim Thompson, Muscogee language specialist, Muscogee (Creek) Nation.

11. opuske. *Opuske* or *apuske* is also called *cold flour* (Debo 303).

13. indistinct tone. According to Speck, the shamans from Taskigi Town blow through a tube into an herb mixture in a pot. This is known as "blowing medicine." The blowing, which is done between the stanzas of songs that go with the herbs in the medicine, strengthens the medicine until it is stronger than the illness (121).

14. busk! Callahan describes the Green Corn ceremony, called Páskida (act of fasting); non-Indians called it a busk, a corruption of Boosketah, a fast held when the corn was large enough for roasting ears, the last of July or first of August. No one was to taste the new corn or other designated foods until the ceremony concluded. The ceremony lasted four or eight days. Swanton summarizes various accounts of this ceremony in "Religious Beliefs" 546–614. See also Speck 137–44; Hewitt 150–53; Debo 21–22.

17. healthy people. The men fasted and drank a medicine to induce vomiting, which purified their bodies for the reception of the maturing crops and ripening fruits. The physic was made from the yaupon or Gulf holly (*Ilex vomitoria*), which the Muscogees called *ussi*; the red willow or *micco hoyanidja* (king of purgers); the button-snake-root (*Eryngium yuccaefolium*) or *passu*; and other plants. The last two were sacred to the Taskigi Muscogees because they were given by the Master of Breath as purifiers and insurers of good health, making them free from possession by harmful spirits. Hewitt notes that the women and children merely washed their hands and faces in it (150). According to Speck, the Muscogees of Hickory Ground near Henryetta, Oklahoma, allowed women to take the emetic (137–38). During the morning, people carried home some of the medicine for the sick. The men remained in the ceremonial square during most

of the celebration. Although women were sometimes admitted to the dancing, most of the time they were excluded (Debo 21).

17. feast to-morrow. Callahan omits the *pókidjida* or racket ball game that was part of the celebrations at some towns. At Taskigi, it had lost its ritual meaning and was done for amusement and betting. (Speck 142–43).

22. 'light fantastic.' "Come and trip it as ye go / On the light fantastic toe." John Milton (1608–74), "L'Allegro," lines 33–34.

22. "human eyes!" John Greenleaf Whittier (1807–92), "Maud Muller," lines 105–6.

23. *vade mecum.* Walking or traveling companion.

26. comfort him. Although at this time some of the older Indians still buried their dead under the floor, most placed them in a family cemetery close to the home. Christians buried their dead in a churchyard, where a small house was erected over the grave. The funeral lasted four days because the spirit was thought to remain in the vicinity for that period of time. In traditional observances, the neighbors remained at the house, carrying out various formulas for the welfare of the dead. In Christian services, the body was carried to the church, where the community joined in songs and prayers. Tobacco, food, clothing, and cherished possessions of the deceased were buried with the body or placed in the house over the grave. The Muscogees at Taskigi kindled a fire at the head of the grave, which relatives tended for four days until the soul reached the sky (Speck 119; Debo 301. Swanton provides various accounts of Muscogee burial customs in "Social Organization" 388 ff.).

27. turned homewards. This practice occurred immediately after burial of the corpse (Swanton, "Religious Beliefs" 395).

30. Samilla. Neither Daniel F. Littlefield Jr. nor I can locate this town.

31. 'oration against Cataline.' Denied a consulship in 65 B.C., an embittered Lucius Sergius Catilina (b. 108 B.C.) plotted to murder the incoming consuls. After he was acquitted of these charges, Cataline

ran again, only to be defeated by Marcus Tullius Cicero (106–43 B.C.) in 63 B.C. He then organized a widespread conspiracy to take over the government, which Cicero, supported by a Senate decree, tried to stop. Cicero attacked Cataline openly in the Senate on 8 November and gave four orations against his enemy. Cataline's forces were annihilated in 62 B.C.

33. 'they lie.' I am unable to locate the source of this quotation.

38. rocks and shells. Callahan bases her description of Keithly College on the Wesleyan Female Institute, Staunton, Virginia, which had a fountain in its front yard. Originally the home of John Cochran, the school was located on top of John Street hill; a four-story addition greatly expanded its facilities. The grounds were "richly adorned and beautified by walks, evergreens, flowers, trees and groves, affording the most delightful retreat for sportive exercise and healthful recreation" (Hamrick 16, 25, 29).

45. that union. Callahan was a member of the Women's Christian Temperance Union (WCTU), whose first convention in Indian Territory was held in Muskogee in July 1888 (See Foreman, "Mrs. Laura E. Harsha" 183).

45. *every* respect. During the 1890s, women increasingly pressed for equality and suffrage. Between 1867 and 1918, states held fifty-six referendum campaigns on suffrage (Flexner 147). Not until 1920 did women gain the right to vote.

48. missionary work? Lucy Ware Webb Hayes (1831–79). The decision of President Rutherford B. Hayes and Lucy not to serve alcohol at White House dinners was widely praised by the religious press and temperance organizations. Over Lucy's objections, the WCTU in 1880 campaigned to raise money to have her portrait painted for the White House. It was presented on 8 March 1881, after President James A. Garfield was inaugurated. In late 1880, she reluctantly agreed to become president of the Woman's Home Missionary Society of the Methodist Episcopal Church, serving until her death. More comfortable in the traditional role as wife and mother, Lucy never commented

on women's suffrage and professional education for women (Geer 148–50, 220–24, 254–55, 168–69). Frances E. Willard praised the First Lady for replacing "the dinner with its wine glasses by the stately and elegant reception" in *Glimpses of Fifty Years*, which may be Callahan's source (333).

48. 'uncrowned queen.' Willard (1839–98) became president of the national WCTU in 1879. Neither Alfred Epstein, librarian of the Frances E. Willard Memorial Library, Evanston, Illinois, nor I can identify the author of the first quotation. According to Earhart, a Canadian woman coined the phrase "the Uncrowned Queen of America," which Willard was frequently called (380). Bernie Babcock used it as the title for her biography for young people: *An Uncrowned Queen: The Story of Frances E. Willard.*

49. "and born," I am unable to identify this quotation.

49. "as one." Lines from Friedrich Halm, Baron von Münch-Bellinghausen (1806–71), *Der Sohn der Wildnis*, act 2 (1842); translated by Maria Lovell as *Ingomar the Barbarian* (1854). Like Lovell, Callahan uses the lines as a repeated refrain.

50. Robert. The reference is clearly to Robin, whose name may be a diminutive for Robert. There are no other references to him as Robert.

52. 'the government.' John Willock Noble (1831–1912), soldier and lawyer, served as secretary of the interior under President William Henry Harrison from 1889 to 1893. Callahan quotes from an editorial in the *Muskogee Daily Phoenix* 4 December 1890, 4.1. Noble's statements appeared in the "Annual Report of the Secretary of the Interior" dated 1 November 1890. In the section on " 'Wild West' Shows," Noble concluded that Indians had "greatly lost" by being taken off the reservation for exhibition. Consequently he stated that "if some act of Congress were passed forbidding any person or corporation to take into employment or under control any American Indian, it would be of much assistance to the Department in enforcing this policy" (xlvii).

On 29 March 1889, the commissioner of Indian affairs issued a notice that all cattle and livestock owned by non-Indians be removed not later than 19 September 1890. Although Noble extended the deadlines for removal granted to non-Indian owners, he reiterated the principle that "this policy of exclusion is still deemed the best for all interests involved" (xxxvii). With regard to allotment, Noble commented that "it is also worthy of consideration whether the period now allowed the tribe to determine whether it will receive allotments should be put under control of the President; so that if he deems it proper in any particular case he may shorten the time for exercising the choice, for as the law stands many tribes give no attention to the subject and delay unreasonably all negotiations" (xxvi). In the section of the report on "Indian Contracts with Attorneys," Noble stated that "it is appropriate in connection with the foregoing cessions to speak of those contracts made by Indian tribes with lawyers and often unprofessional men to secure their services in obtaining the allowance of certain claims, or to aid in certain negotiations, the fee or compensation being usually contingent upon success" (xxiv). The Secretary objected to this practice on the grounds that although the tribes received a small percentage of the sums awarded, they paid very large compensation to the lawyers. For him, the issue was an affair between the "guardian and the ward" over fair compensation. Noble declared that the sole motive of the commissioners, selected for their "worth and intelligence" and compensated only to "meet their expenses," is "to do justice by the Indians as well as to the nation" (xxiv–v).

52. 'Poor Lo!' Alexander Pope (1688–1744), "An Essay on Man," line 99: "Lo, the poor Indian!"

58. the cause. In 1823, George Gordon (Noel) Byron, Lord Byron, (1788–1824) became the agent of the London Greek Committee to aid the Greeks in the war of independence from the Turks. He contributed four thousand pounds of his own money and went to Greece to plan an attack on the Turkish-held fortress of Lepanto,

command and pay a group of soldiers, and unite quarreling factions of eastern and western Greeks. He died in Greece as a result of severe fever, aggravated by the bleeding administered by his doctors.

59. 'even my people, Israel.' Callahan paraphrases 2 Samuel 3.18: "By the hand of my servant David, I will save my people Israel out of the hand of the Philistines, and out of the hand of all enemies."

61. Pocahontas . . . John Smith. Pocahontas (ca. 1595–1617), daughter of Chief Powhatan, befriended British colonists and taught Captain John Smith her language. According to the legend, first recounted by Smith in his *Generall Historie* (1624), he was taken prisoner in 1607 and was about to be killed by Powhatan, when Pocahontas (then eleven or twelve) seized his head in her arms and saved his life. After the incident she became even more attached to the colonists. Abducted by the English in 1613, she became a Christian convert, took the name of Rebecca, married John Rolfe in 1614, and bore a son in 1615. The next year she accompanied Rolfe to England, where she died in 1617 just before they were to sail back to the New World.

62. 'good days are done.' Alfred, Lord Tennyson (1809–92), "Lancelot and Elaine," *Idylls of the King*, line 941.

73. 'Messiah at dawn.' Cf. the report in the 27 November 1890 issue of the *Muskogee Daily Phoenix* that the Sioux and allied bands had "for months past engaged in ghost dances and their frenzy has been wrought to such a point that they are scarcely accountable for their actions" (4.2).

73. Hadjo. A reference to the name Harjo.

85. "all understanding." Philippeans 4.7: "And the peace of God, which passeth all understanding, shall keep your hearts and minds through Jesus Christ."

86. 'I will repay.' Romans 12.19: "Vengence *is* mine, I will repay, saith the Lord."

86. Miscona. This is not a Sioux name. Information provided by Beatrice Medicine and Harvey Markowitz.

88. terrible ride. On 18 April 1775, Paul Revere (1735–1818), a craftsman and industrialist, rode to warn the Massachusetts colonists of the approaching British troops. Philip Henry Sheridan (1831–88) was a brilliant military campaigner. Callahan undoubtedly alludes to Sheridan's order that all means of subsistence for the Confederates be destroyed as Union forces marched through the South, an act that has often been censured. He was made a brigadier general shortly after he issued the order.

90. beloved dead. Rizpah was a concubine of the biblical King Saul. When a famine was attributed to the deceased Saul's covenant with the Gibeonites, David gave Rizpah's two sons and five other descendants of Saul to the Gibeonites in expiation. After the Gibeonites executed them, Rizpah guarded the bodies day and night until rain returned. Inspired by her example, David publicly buried Saul and Jonathan. See 2 Samuel 3 and 21.

92. mothers' bosoms. The *St. Louis Republic* reported on 4 January 1891 that "two tiny Indian babies, neither of them over three months old, were found alive, each beside the dead body of its mother" (6.3). According to Renée Sansom Flood, five babies under a year old were rescued by burial parties. Others lived through the ordeal, rescued by men from the Ghost Dance bands. The most famous of these was Zitkala Nuni or "Lost Bird," whose tragic biography Flood has written in *Lost Bird of Wounded Knee* (60).

95. Horda. This is not a Sioux name. Information provided by Beatrice Medicine and Harvey Markowitz.

96. subsistence for himself. According to the *Muskogee Daily Phoenix* (7 August 1890, 1.2) the "condition and complaints of ill-treatment" made by Indians recently returned from Buffalo Bill's and other Wild West shows then in Europe were outlined in a letter sent by General James O'Beirne to Thomas J. Morgan, commissioner of Indian affairs. O'Beirne suggested that the United States authorities investigate. The Bureau of Indian Affairs looked into the matter. Yost comments that despite "ample proof that the Indians were well

fed, well used, well paid, and happy, the rumors persisted in eastern American newspapers" (224).

98. "hell itself." I have been unable to find this issue of the *Telephone*.

100. greatest dispatch. The *St. Louis Republic*'s account of 31 December exemplifies the reaction Callahan describes. It exults over how the Indians were mowed down by Hotchkiss guns: "It must have been an inspiring spectacle. How proud the gentlemen of West Point who did their share in it must be of the noble profession which makes them the instruments of Messrs. HARRISON and NOBLE in this grand and glorious work!" The report noted that although some army men were killed, their lives were cheap: "We get many of them in the slums of the cities after their degradation has unfitted them for citizenship, and if the Indians kill a few of them we can afford to stand that score as long as they exterminate the Indians. . . . Our noble and chivalric gentlemen from West Point showed themselves worthy of their cause. . . . 'Oh, how we slaughtered them,' writes the enthusiastic correspondent of *The Republic* on the ground." The account concludes, "A few more displays of heroism like that at Wounded Knee Creek and there will not be a blanket Indian, squaw or pappoose left to disfigure the face of the continent" (6.2–3).

101. "sad but true." Callahan quotes from the *Cherokee Telephone* (Tahlequah, Cherokee Nation) 22 January 1891, 2.1.

101. 'know them.' "Ye shall know them by their fruits." Matthew 7.16.

101. 'Indian troubles.' On 16 December 1890, the *St. Louis Republic* reported that President Benjamin Harrison said "he regarded Sitting Bull as the great disturbing element in his tribe, and now that he was out of the way he hoped that a settlement of the difficulties could be reached without further trouble or bloodshed" (1.2–3). The interview originally appeared in the *New York Herald* (see Vestal 310).

Obvious spelling and punctuation errors have been silently corrected.

WORKS CITED AND
RECOMMENDED READING

ABBREVIATIONS

ARBAE *Annual Report of the Bureau of American Ethnology*
BBAE   *Bulletin of the Bureau of American Ethnology*
CO   *Chronicles of Oklahoma*
MAAA   *Memoirs of the American Anthropological Association*

"Appendix, Samuel Benton Callahan." CO 33 (1955): 314–15.

Babcock, Bernie. *An Uncrowned Queen: The Story of Frances E. Willard Told for Young People*. Chicago: Revell, 1902.

Bakhtin, Mikhail M. *The Dialogic Imagination: Four Essays*. Trans. Caryl Emerson and Michael Holquist. Ed. Michael Holquist. Austin: U Texas P, 1981.

Banta, Martha. "They Shall Have Faces, Minds, and (One Day) Flesh: Women in Late Nineteenth-Century and Early Twentieth-Century American Literature." *What Manner of Woman: Essays on English and American Life and Literature*. Ed. Marlene Springer. New York: New York UP, 1977.

Baym, Nina. *Women's Fiction: A Guide to Novels by and about Women in America, 1820–1870*. Ithaca: Cornell University Press, 1978.

Berlant, Lauren. "The Female Woman: Fanny Fern and the Form of Sentiment." *The Culture of Sentiment: Race, Gender, and Sentimentality in Nineteenth-Century America*. Ed. Shirley Samuels. New York: Oxford UP, 1992.

Brown, David J., ed. *Staunton, Virginia: A Pictorial History*. Staunton VA: Historic Staunton Foundation, 1985.

Champagne, Duane. *Social Order and Political Change: Constitutional Governments among the Cherokee, the Choctaw, the Chickasaw, and the Creek*. Stanford: Stanford UP, 1992.

Debo, Angie. *The Road to Disappearance: A History of the Creek Indians*. Civilization of the American Indian Series 22. Norman: U Oklahoma P, 1941.

Dorris, Michael. "Modoc Sketches." *Journal of the Modoc County Historical Society* 12 (1990): 161–73.

Douglas, Ann. *The Feminization of American Culture*. New York: Knopf, 1977. New York: Doubleday, 1988.

Earhart, Mary. *Frances Willard: From Prayers to Politics*. Chicago: U Chicago P, 1944.

Flexner, Eleanor. *Century of Struggle: The Woman's Rights Movement in the United States*. Cambridge: Harvard UP, 1950, 1970.

Flood, Renée Sansom. *Lost Bird of Wounded Knee: Spirit of the Lakota*. New York: Scribner, 1995.

Foreman, Carolyn Thomas. "Mrs. Laura E. Harsha." CO 18.2 (1940): 182–84.

———. "S. Alice Callahan: Author of *Wynema, A Child of the Forest*." CO 33 (1955): 306–15, 549.

Foreman, Grant. *Muskogee: The Biography of an Oklahoma Town*. St. Louis: privately printed, 1945.

Geer, Emily Apt. *First Lady: The Life of Lucy Webb Hayes*. Kent, OH: Rutherford Hayes Presidential Center/Kent State UP, 1984.

Green, Michael D. *The Politics of Indian Removal: Creek Government and Society in Crisis*. Lincoln: U Nebraska P, 1982.

Griswold, Robert. "Anglo Women and Domestic Ideology in the American West in Nineteenth and Early Twentieth Centuries." *Western Women: Their Land, Their Lives*. Ed. Lillian Schlissel, Vicki L. Ruiz, and Janice Monk. Albuquerque: U New Mexico P, 1988.

Hamrick, Martha Peyton. "The Wesleyan Female Institute." *Augusta Historical Bulletin* (Augusta County [VA] Historical Society) 6.1 (1970): 17–34.

Hewitt, J. N. B. "Notes on the Creek Indians." Ed. John R. Swanton. BBAE 123, Anthropological Papers 10 (1939).

Kolodny, Annette. *The Land before Her: Fantasy and Experience of the American Frontiers, 1630–1860.* Chapel Hill: U North Carolina P, 1984.

Littlefield, Daniel F., Jr. Introduction. *The Fus Fixico Letters.* By Alexander Posey. Ed. Daniel F. Littlefield Jr. and Carol A. Petty Hunter. Foreword by A. LaVonne Brown Ruoff. Lincoln: U Nebraska P, 1993.

Littlefield, Daniel F., Jr., and James W. Parins. *American Indian and Alaska Native Newspapers and Periodicals, 1826–1924.* Westport CT: Greenwood, 1984.

Martin, Joel W. *Sacred Revolt: The Muskogees' Struggle for a New World.* Boston: Beacon, 1991.

Meacham, Alfred B. *Wigwam and War-Path; or the Royal Chief in Chains.* 2nd ed., rev. Boston: Dale, 1875.

———. *Wi-ne-ma (the Woman Chief) and Her People.* 1876. New York: AMS, 1980.

Murray, Keith A. *The Modocs and Their War.* Norman: U Oklahoma P, 1959, 1965.

Pasco, Peggy. *Relations of Rescue: The Search for Female Moral Authority in the American West, 1874–1939.* New York: Oxford UP, 1990.

Ruoff, A. LaVonne Brown. *American Indian Literatures: An Introduction, Bibliographic Review, and Selected Bibliography.* New York: Modern Language Association, 1990.

Showalter, Elaine. *A Literature of Their Own: British Women Novelists from Brontë to Lessing.* Princeton: Princeton UP, 1977.

Speck, Frank G. "The Creek Indians of Taskigi Town." MAAA 2 (1907–15): 99–164. Rpt. New York: Kraus, 1964.

Swanton, John R. "The Green Corn Dance." CO 10.11 (1932): 170–95.

———. "Religious Beliefs and Medical Practices of the Creek Indians." ARBAE 42 (1924–25): 473–672.

———. "Social Organization and Social Usages of the Indians of the Creek Confederacy." ARBAE 42 (1924–25): 23–472.

Tompkins, Jane. *Sensational Designs: The Cultural Work of American Fiction, 1790–1860*. New York: Oxford UP, 1985.

Tyler, S. Lyman. *A History of Indian Policy*. Washington DC: Bureau of Indian Affairs, U.S. Dept. of Interior, 1973.

Utley, Robert M. *The Lance and the Shield: The Life and Times of Sitting Bull*. New York: Holt, 1993. New York: Ballentine, 1994.

———. *The Last Days of the Sioux Nation*. New Haven: Yale UP, 1963, 1966.

Vestal, Stanley. *Sitting Bull: Champion of the Sioux*. Norman: U Oklahoma P, 1957.

Washburn, Wilcomb E. *The Indian in America*. New York: Harper, 1975.

Weir, Sybil. "A Bacchante Invades the American Home: The Disappearance of the Sentimental Heroine, 1890–1910." *American Literature, Culture, and Ideology: Essays in Memory of Henry Nash Smith*. Ed. Beverly R. Voloshin. American University Studies: American Literature. Series 24, Vol. 8. New York: Peter Lang, 1990.

Willard, Frances. *Glimpses of Fifty Years: The Autobiography of an American Woman*. Chicago: Women's Christian Temperance Union, 1889.

Yost, Nellie Snyder. *Buffalo Bill: His Family, Friends, Fame, Failures, and Fortunes*. Chicago: Swallow, 1979.

Ziff, Larzer. *The American 1890s: Life and Times of a Lost Generation*. Lincoln: U Nebraska P, 1966.